I0583022

THE eSMITH EYE STORY

by

GranRan

BOOK TWO:
One Eye Open

Published by NuSaga Press

P.O. Box 689

Lowell, NC 28098

All Standard Print editions contain black and white illustrations to offset cost.

For color illustrations see the Large Print edition, the eBook version, or the Hardback edition where available.

This collection is a work of fantasy, all characters, settings, events, etc. are based upon the author's imagination and any product that resembles a real person, place, or thing is purely coincidental.

Cover and illustrations provided by NuSaga Press 2022

THE eSMITH EYE STORY

First Printing April 2022

ISBN: 978-0-9974317-9-7

DEDICATION

To Tammy Marie Watkins Miller White
my wife of thirty plus years.
You are an amazing person.

Other Books by GranRan:

The Magical Meniscus

**The eSmith Short Tales:
Fables & Stories from Fairytale Land**

TABLE OF CONTENTS

BOOK TWO: ONE EYE OPEN

CHAPTER ONE

TWO ONE-EYED, RED JACKALS

The Predator's Tavern was hopping, and everyone was having a good time, except for the gray fox, eSmith. He had just lost his foxy fox to another. He felt betrayed by Roxie after all he had done. How many times had he faced death to get that barter to free her? His blood boiled at the thought of how she used him. He had always been on the edge of compassion, but Roxie changed all that for him.

"That's what compassion gets you," he hissed, vowing never to show a lick of compassion for anyone that did not profit him first.

eSmith growled at anyone approaching him about a good time. He shoved and grunted those who thought they knew better. He showed a few of those predators his claws. He still could not accept Roxy running off with that no-account bartender, Charlie. The incident had made him the laughingstock of the tavern.

"Give me a bottle of the best stuff you have," he barked in the face of the new bartender. He was not sure if he liked this bartender any better than the last one—the one who ran off with Roxie. He growled at the wolf serving up drinks anyway. He tried to forget her, but no matter how much he consumed, he could not forget those crystal blue eyes and her lovely gold-tipped red brush. He started up a cigar.

"Smoking is a bad habit," protested one brash vixen, waving her paws to clear the air.

"Mind your own business," barked eSmith. "Hypocrites."

7

"Lung cancer is the leading cause of cancer deaths," howled another predator.

eSmith slammed down his bottle and jumped on top of the bar. "Listen up!"

The music died down, and everyone turned to the gray fox.

He paced the planks. "Of all my faults, you've chosen to pick on me about my smoking habit. What about my drinking habit? Or my gambling? Or my vixen-izing? Why aren't they as bad as smoking?"

"A breathing machine," hissed Crandall.

"True enough, but can't we get over this, 'smoking is a bad habit' crap?" I know it's bad, like all my habits. Do I need to remind each of you about your bad habits?"

"Leave him alone," barked one predator.

Everyone turned away; eSmith grabbed a bottle and found a quiet corner.

"Go away," he growled when folks came begging. He drank on, but it did not make him feel better. He doubted if anything could make him feel better.

eSmith finished the bottle and went for another.

"Hey, watch where you are going!" he hissed at the arctic fox standing at the bar.

Crandall turned about and barked, "Don't know what you're talking about."

"You keep talking, and you'll get me," snarled eSmith, slamming down his drink.

"I don't want no trouble," barked Crandall. "I didn't know he was your father,"

Dropping the bottle, eSmith howled at the moon and jumped on the arctic fox.

"What's going on?" Crandall fought him off, knocking eSmith to the ground.

The crowd parted as the gray fox hit the dirt. He rolled over and stood on all fours.

"I don't want to fight," barked the arctic fox.

"I do!" eSmith jumped him.

Crandall sent the gray fox flying. "Sorry for your loss, but you're barking at the wrong fox here. I didn't kill your father, nor did I take your foxy fox."

eSmith dove at the arctic fox. Crandall slammed him into the wall before dropping him to the ground. He stepped back, barking, "I mean you no harm."

Hissing, eSmith slowly rose, too tired to fight. He accepted that Crandall was more talented in self-defense.

"Are you okay?" Crandall asked.

"Screw you," snarled eSmith. Pushing aside folks, he staggered back to the bar for another battle.

***

After a few more drinks, eSmith decided to get back in the game. He headed for the poker table. He watched the game unfold. Several mutts were in the game, including two coyotes, a brown bear, a hyena, and a greyhound. And then there was Zeke. The brown and gray wolf shuffled the cards. A gleam of triumph in his eyed, he barked, "Miss her already."

Growling at the remark, eSmith patted his pockets, stuffed with winnings. This wolf needed a lesson. And he intended to deliver that lesson.

He liked cards as much as playing billiards, especially when he felt lucky, but he did not feel lucky right now. In fact, he didn't feel anything at the moment. So, he lost one match after another without a thought; instead, he ordered more beer.

"Cards anyone?" snarled Zeke, a glitter of triumph sparkling in his eye. He blew smoke in the gray fox's face.

"Nasty," snarled eSmith. Playing it off, he still felt the rage burning inside. And the urge to smoke one had to be snuffed out. Lady Luck had turned a blind eye to his needs. He continued to lose. Anteing up for the next match, he was determined not to feel anything, let alone compassion.

Zeke nodded to his muscle dog, his most trusting comrade, Rocky. The grayish-black Rottweiler with bulging shoulders and a low mean growl acknowledged the gesture.

"Got you covered, boss," snarled Rocky. "Get him a beer."

The greyhound shuffled the deck and dealt out the cards.

eSmith studied his cards: two axes, three diamonds, one of which was a king. Nothing. He tossed in his cards and chugged on his beer.

The greyhound had three of a kind and the best cards again.

"He wins a lot!" snarled the hyena, glaring at the greyhound.

The greyhound woofed, "I don't need luck."

He scooped up the pile of gems and gold trinkets.

"Well, I do," grumbled eSmith, wondering where his Lady Luck was hiding. Had he done something to offend her, he wondered what it could have been. Why did Lady Luck have to be a female, a vixen? Perhaps it was her? Roxie must have stabbed him in the back with bad luck. Was he not the one unjustly treated? He tossed away his cards.

"Ante up," barked Zeke. He shuffled the cards and dealt them out.

The match played out the same as the last few.

"I win again," cheered the greyhound. He scooped up his winnings. An ace fell from his shirt pocket onto the table. He quickly scooped it up.

"I saw that!" growled the brown bear. "He cheated."

"That's a lie!" the greyhound howled.

Rocky grabbed his arm and checked his pockets. The muscle dog pulled out a king of Cobras from an inside pocket and showed it to everyone at the table.

"Cheat!" snarled Zeke. "Get rid of him."

Rocky snatched up the greyhound, dragging him from the chair. He took the dog outside. The greyhound's painful howls ended with the sharp cracking of bones.

"Lucky me," Zeke snarled. He raked the greyhound's winnings into his own pile.

The thugs behind the wolf snarled and chuckled.

"Your deal," barked eSmith. He passed the deck of cards to the coyote to the right.

"Five card stud," yapped the brown coyote. He dealt out the cards; everyone anted up.

Zeke nodded to his most trusting comrade, Rocky.

"Everywhere I look, I see a cheater," barked Zeke, his eyes settling on eSmith. He snatched up the cards and dealt out a round of seven-card stud. Winning, he raked in the pot. "I sure miss my foxy fox, Roxie."

eSmith glared back at him.

The brown and gray wolf elbowed the muscle dog, Rocky, in the side and yapped, "She's mighty fine that one."

Rocky grunted at the remark.

Studying his cards, the gray fox played ignorant, indifferent would be best; he told himself to act the same way as when she strutted about getting predators to buy drinks.

"She has one mighty fine brush," barked Zeke.

eSmith snorted at Zeke's crude remarks. It was all a distraction, he kept telling himself. For some reason, Lady Luck was not around, so he kept losing barter. He ordered another beer from the wolf tending bar and notified Wild Bill to bring his remaining winnings.

"Seven-card stud, jackals wild," barked Zeke.

The red coyote snarled, "My kind of game."

The hyena barked, "Sounds good."

Everyone anted up and checked their cards. The cards showed favor for the coyote, so eSmith folded early on that hand, leaving Zeke and the red coyote to settle up things.

"Looks like I win," said the red coyote, showing three of a kind.

"Great," snapped the brown bear. He tossed in his cards.

Rocky grabbed the coyote's arm and checked his pockets. He found several cards up the red coyote's shirt sleeves. "He's been cheating too."

"Take him out back. Show him what happens to cheaters," Zeke ordered.

Everyone watched the coyote put up a fight until Rocky slapped him down. The muscle dog dragged the unconscious coyote outside.

eSmith heard a sharp yelp from the red coyote, and the predator was never heard from again. For some reason, the silence made him think of Roxie. It made him miss her even more.

Zeke growled at the silver fox playing the piano. The piano player rapped out several upbeat tunes to distract the crowd, including the ever-popular tune, "That's Not Me Barking at the Moon."

Still on a losing streak, eSmith lost the next match of stud to the brown wolf.

"I'm out," hissed the hyena. He staggered away from the table.

eSmith eyed his stack: two gold ingots, four rubies, and five sapphires. Pitiful. He would be out of barter in another few rounds.

Other predators closed in around them, watching the outcome of the final game.

"Back up there," screamed Wild Bill from the bar. "Give them some room."

The spectators moved back and kept the talk to a minimum.

eSmith grappled with his meager stack of winnings. It

was not looking good. Soon, all his winnings would be gone.

"Are you in?" Zeke confronted him, "loser."

Snarling, the gray fox felt low and mean. She did that. He understood that easily enough. He drank more beer and smoked his cigar, trying not to think of her. He barked. "Why not?"

"Ante up," Zeke tossed in a gold nugget. "Now!"

"There!" eSmith tossed in his barter. He picked up the deck of cards. He refused to cheat, so he played his game honestly, and he continued to lose.

The brown and gray wolf snorted lightly. Several husky mutts behind him backed up. Zeke shifted his stare to the gray fox. "Deal."

"Good," snarled eSmith. He stared down the bigger predator a moment, then picked up the deck of cards. "Five Card Stud."

Zeke puffed on a cigar until its tip glowed cherry hot. "Sure, miss that red hot brush."

eSmith snarled for Zeke had finally gotten on his last nerve. That arrogant wolf had yet to learn his lesson. He decided to cheat once to teach Zeke that lesson.

He soon had picked up a spare one-eyed, red jackal. Shuffling the deck, he passed out the cards. "Five-card stud with one-eyed jackals wild."

"You sound confident," snarled Zeke. Checking his cards, he glared at eSmith once he exchanged cards. He laid a black one-eyed jackal on the table next to two Kings. "In case you have any doubt who's going to win. Three of a kind."

Going to the hidden one-eyed, red jackal, eSmith grinned. He laid out his three aces.

"Will that do?" He reached for the winnings.

Zeke snarled at him, "You stink."

"No more than you," he hissed.

eSmith raked in the winnings. Leaning over the table, he scooped up the loot, overturning the cards in the process. A second one-eyed, red jackal popped out. "Huh, what are the chances?"

"Two one-eyed, red jackals! You're a crook!" barked Zeke, giving his most trusting comrade, Rocky, the sign. "Get him!"

The muscle dog growled at eSmith; the gray fox fanned apart the cards in Rocky's face, distracting him.

"Cheater!" howled Zeke.

"I am not!" snapped eSmith. "Well, just this once. Thought you needed a lesson."

Rocky moved in, growling, snarling, grabbing for him.

"Wow! Not on a first date," eSmith yelped, scooping up his winnings.

Rocky and the other predators closed in. They jumped him. Four of them butted heads as they grabbed for the Sly One.

eSmith raked Zeke's winnings into his shirt and slid off the chair. He hit the ground and wormed his way from under the pile of bodies, leaving behind a trail of trinkets. Five of the predators smashed heads into each other, grabbing for him or the trinkets he had left behind.

Rocky pushed and shoved the others out of his way.

eSmith scurried mouse-like toward the exit; Zeke jumped on top of the table and barked, "What're you doing?"

His gang stopped fighting each other and looked up at the brown and gray wolf.

"He's over there!" snarled Zeke, pointed towards the cavern's exit.

The gang turned in eSmith's direction; He stopped

creeping to look around at them. Grinning slyly, the gray fox dashed for the exit.

The pack charged after him, running into each other again.

He kept five steps ahead of the Rottweiler. He slammed shut the tavern doors and held them shut. Thump! Thump! Thump! Thump!

"Oh, that had to hurt!" he hissed.

"Hey, what are you doing?" growled the bouncer, Blackie.

"Nothing." eSmith released his hold on the doors and scrambled for the forbidden forest. He made the tree line with his winnings before they picked up his scent and began trailing him.

CHAPTER TWO

EYESORE

Smith kicked back on a grassy knoll under a mimosa, chewed on a piece of sweetgrass, and reflected on the chase. He had led them on a merry journey through the countryside. For him, this over-the-hill-and-dale fox chase led nowhere. In fact, they ended up where they began. Usually, he would put as much distance between himself and the posse, but Zeke's posse were all amateurs. None of them could track a buffalo, let alone a fox. They were nothing like Brutus and the huntsman. No need to worry there, he grinned slyly.

Once he set a few traps, eSmith waited for them to catch up. He had created a false trail and covered up a narrow, steep ravine with old limbs and branches. He sprinkled a few sticks and leaves about to conceal any tracks before he climbed a tree near that location.

The crew ran blindly into the trap. Two fell inside; the bulldog known as Chuck climbed out, but the short-eared, long-snouted hound known as Jones sprained his front right paw in the fall. It took Jones a moment to climb out.

Massaging his hurt paw, Jones growled, "He's a clever one."

"Quit crying, pup and keep up," snarled Rocky.

"Hey, that rhymes," woofed Chuck.

The muscle dog growled at him.

Resting in the tree high above the posse, eSmith listened to them until his stomach rumbled. He spotted several bird nests hiding among its branches. Perhaps dinner? Or breakfast? He rubbed his lean belly and felt it growl back.

He checked the nearest bird's nest, but there were no eggs. So, he climbed higher, reaching a squirrel's nest. He searched all levels; the dray was empty. Up another branch, a sparrow's nest held old eggshells scattered about and one remaining egg: unbroken. He grabbed it and tossed it into his mouth.

The posse gathered under the tree where he was hiding. He froze for fear they would detect him, high above them.

Silently, he chomped down on the egg and swallowed. A foul-tasting stench filled his mouth. It turned his stomach sour. His ears felt like they were going to pop. The gray fox vented through his nostrils, but it hurt. eSmith wanted to throw up the egg but feared discovery. He clamped both paws about his snout, shaking a branch. He hoped those below had not seen the movement. He remained silent and immobile. His face turned from green to ash gray.

"This way," directed Zeke. The wolf stopped directly below him. "He's near, I feel it."

Rocky picked up the other trail. "You sure it's not this one? Smells like the trail to me."

"There's two trails," bayed Chuck.

"Okay," hissed Zeke. He sniffed along both trails. "You take Chuck and Jones and follow that one. I'll check this one. One of these will end sooner or later."

Finally, the group split up and eSmith spit out the rotten egg. He grabbed his stomach and threw up again. It made him dizzy. He drank at a local stream and rested, but he did not feel any better. He felt worse, so he ate tree bark and grass to settle his aching belly. He should have known that egg was bad; the eggshells alone should have warned him.

Divided into two groups, they tracked both trails to

eSmith's delight. He decided to track Rocky and his crew first, trailing after them. He had to slow up, for they often lost the trail, a trail any good tracker could have taken at a trot.

Rocky and his crew tracked him across the valley, eventually bringing them to a steep narrow incline leading to a tall rocky summit.

Rocky and Chuck scouted out the base until Jones hobbled up on his sore leg. Panting, the short-eared long-snouted hound dropped to the ground next to Chuck. "Finally, here."

Rocky confronted him. "Get up there and check."

"What?" barked Jones, rubbing his sore leg.

"You pull your weight or get out," snarled Rocky.

"I'll do it." Jones stood on his sore leg and climbed the steep rocky incline. The long-snouted hound fell over the side, trying to track him, landing on his back and side.

"Ouch!" Jones whined in pain.

"Are you okay?" inquired his friend, the bulldog, Chuck.

"No. I'm out," Jones howled, grabbing his leg. "I'm heading back."

"Good luck," Chuck barked, patting Jones on the shoulder. "See you back at the tavern."

"Yeah, you too," barked Jones. He limped east towards Wizard Peak.

"Whiner," snarled the muscle dog. Rocky tapped the bulldog on the shoulder and pointed toward the top of the rocky mound. "Go check it out."

eSmith's spirit soared. It was working!

Chuck made the top of the rocky summit and returned to report. "He's gone or never there. I saw no signs."

"Let's get up with the boss," barked the muscle dog. Rocky picked up the trail of Zeke and the others. Chuck followed him with eSmith trailing them.

Zeke, too, had little success in locating the gray fox with his crew. The second trail led to a rocky outcrop that they could not climb. "The trail ends here. Find a way up."

The posse spread out to find access to the top while Zeke rested.

Rocky's group arrived and aided in the search.

eSmith scaled a mighty maple tree to a lofty branch and leaped onto a cliff nearby. He scrambled to the top before anyone noticed.

The posse rushed about seeking clues or access to the top of the outcropping.

"Find a way up yet?" Zeke asked Rocky once he woke up.

"Not yet, Boss," yapped the muscle dog arriving at the small steam.

Zeke took a few breaths and barked, "Go around the cliff."

"That'll take most of the day." Rocky stopped halfway across the small stream to drink.

He's right in that regard, eSmith hissed in delight. He enjoyed their struggle to catch him. He kicked away a few loose stones.

The stones pelted Zeke and his minions in the face; rock dust fell into their eyes.

"What's that?" howled Chuck. He scratched at his eyes.

The cunning wolf moved away from the cliff, wiping the rock dust from his eyes. "Yeah, he's up there."

"I can't see anything," yapped one of the moguls in the posse.

"It's him!" snarled Zeke, rubbing his eye. He headed for the stream.

"He's an eyesore," whined Chuck.

"I want him!" Zeke snarled, wading into the steam. He shoved his head under the water to clear the rock dust from his eyes. He shook dry and did it again.

The bulldog did the same.

Kicking back, the gray fox listened to them bicker. Rocky kept cutting them off when one of them made a silly suggestion.

While Zeke went to relieve himself, the posse spread out along the riverbank; from far across the flatland movement drew their attention. "Who's that?"

"Did someone send for help?" howled one of Zeke's thugs.

"We don't need help from any stranger, understand?" snarled Rocky, sniffing out the crew. They agreed with the muscle dog.

"Ah, he's finally arrived," Zeke barked once he caught up with the others.

"Who is it?" growled Rocky, flexing his muscles.

"Someone who will get us that fox," yapped Zeke. "He's a real brute."

eSmith stomach tightened on the remark. Eyes wide open, he sat upon the cliff: Brutus! The tracker hobbled up. *This is not good*, groaned the gray fox.

The posse grumbled among themselves until the tracker arrived. Brutus was a mix of Doberman and bloodhound. He had a thick neck and barrel chest. Sniffling about, he growled, "I smell him on you now. Or is it your fear of him?"

The posse snarled and snapped at him. "We're not afraid of you."

"I'll hurt you bad," promised Rocky.

Limping about, Brutus sniffed over the posse. He lingered over the muscle dog, snarling. "What are you howling about?"

"You heard me," snapped Rocky. He faced down the tracker.

They stared at each other until Zeke stepped in.

"Hold on! I hired him to find the fox," barked Zeke.

"I was working on it," Rocky assured his boss.

"You had your chance," snarled Brutus. "Get over it."

"I can't work with him," hissed Rocky.

"Learn to," ordered Zeke. "He'll find that gray rat."

eSmith began to hiss at the remark, but fear stayed his tongue. It would give away his location and end the chase early.

"That's why I'm here, Rock-o," snapped Brutus. "To get him."

"Name's Rocky," snarled the muscle dog. "Cripple!"

Brutus snarled at Rocky before turned to the trail.

eSmith withdrew, hoping to find a way out. He needed to get some distance, and the approaching storm may help.

***

To eSmith's bitter disappointment, things had changed for the worse. Brutus led the pack now. That meant Rocky fell to third-in-command. The gray fox hurried along, determined to find a solution. He was not going to be able to outrun them. He needed to approach this from a different angle.

The posse moved much faster with Brutus showing the way. The brute bulled his way past Rocky.

A silly idea popped into his head; he wondered if it could work. Could he turn them on each other? The old "divide and conquer" tactic always worked, more or less.

He stumbled on a cave and strolled into the darkness. His eyes quickly adjusted, and he saw something huddling among the rocks and dried weeds littering the place. It was a black bear. He slid past the sleeping bear and took another exit, emerging high above them.

Brutus stood at the opening of the cave and pointed the way. "He went in there."

"Are you going in there?" demanded Rocky.

"No, I think you need to pick someone," hissed the brute. "Or pick yourself, Rock-o."

"Told you my name," shouted the muscle dog. "It's Rocky!"

"Yeah, yeah," bayed the tracker. He yawned in the muscle dog's face.

Rocky bared teeth, bunched up his muscles, and growled back.

"Chill!" Zeke separated them before he sniffed out the newest member of the posse. He pushed the young mutt toward the entrance and barked. "Go on. Check it out."

The mutt crept toward the dark opening. He stumbled about the darkness until he kicked awake the bear. The bear rose and struck the dog, sending him to the ground. The mauler feasted on the dog as Zeke backed away from the cave.

"We could have done that different," yapped Rocky.

"Small loss," hissed Brutus, shuffling along. "I know he's nearby. He's probably watching us right now."

eSmith backed away from the ledge. Had he been seen?

"I don't see anything." The muscle dog scratched his head.

"Maybe you should open your eyes," Brutus yapped casually.

"I'm tired of this cripple," Rocky barked. "We don't need him, Boss. I'll find the fox."

Brutus hissed, "You couldn't find termites in a pile."

"I'm tired of you," snarled the muscle dog. Rocky got up in the brute's face again.

"Do something about it," Brutus stiffened his hitched leg and spat back in the muscle dog's face, "Coward!"

"You're on!" howled Rocky. He bared fangs.

The gray fox's eyes sparkled, and his ears piqued up as the two circled each other, looking for a weakness. This was going to be good; he grinned slyly.

Limping, Brutus kept his wounded leg away from the muscle dog. He dashed in, attacking Rocky in the side. He knocked silly the muscle dog before he sank teeth in his biceps. Once the tracker latched on, he remained determined not to let go. In fact, Brutus chewed harder and harder until he tasted blood.

With a painful whine, Rocky kicked the brute away.

"Looks like I'm not the only one bleeding," wolfed Brutus. "Sweet."

"We'll see about that," hissed Rocky. He grabbed his bleeding shoulder. The dog had bit into his bicep and nibbled on his triceps too!

They circled again, and once more, the tracker proved victorious. Rocky suffered several vicious bites to his stomach from Brutus. He kicked away the brute.

Brutus knocked the muscle dog to the ground and latched on the dog's throat.

"You don't have to kill him," snarled Zeke, his cold eyes on the wounded muscle dog.

The tracker released the injured dog. Backing away, Brutus returned to the search after barking, "I don't have a problem with that."

"I'll never give in," Rocky howled. "Never!"

"I thought so," Brutus jumped on the muscle dog. He sank his teeth into the dog's neck and latched on until Rocky no longer moved.

"Satisfied?" sneered Zeke.

"Yeah, I think I'm good now," howled the tracker. He sniffed about the bushes, searching for signs.

"That's cold," snarled Chuck.

eSmith cheered in silence. It was working!

"I'm leading now. You're following," barked Brutus. "Understand?"

Chuck shook his head. He walked away, grumbling, "You put that much faith in him?"

"I put my faith in barter," howled Zeke. He looked at the tracker. "Can you find him?"

"Yeah, I will," Brutus assured them. "Quicker than that muscle-head."

"He's howling bad things about Rocky," protested Chuck. Several of the others agreed with the bulldog. They crowded behind him to show their support. The bulldog sneered, "Find the fox and keep your stinking lies to yourself!"

The tracker sniffed the air. "Smells like rain to me."

CHAPTER THREE

BLUE-EYED MONSTERS

It had been raining off and on for nearly six days before the gray fox reached the mighty Rose River. It was flooded. He had not realized it flowed this far south. It must be the west branch, he calculated. Windy rain stabbed him in the face and pelted him from head to paw. He needed to find a way to cross the nearly half--kilometer-wide river.

The current seemed to boil up, a torrent of rapidly moving water and debris. Nevertheless, he continued upriver, seeking a narrow section to cross over.

The storm waters had eaten the soil from under a mighty sequoia tree, uprooting it. The tree spanned the river and made travel much easier. With the wind and rain whipping about him, the gray fox skipped and danced across the river.

Waves of debris piled up against the sequoia while the river ate at its supports, causing the tree to shift. The sudden move made him slip off the tree and fall in.

eSmith splashed about, trying to keep afloat. Swept downstream, he clutched anything floating past. Most did little to help his situation. For some time, he drifted with the current. Logs and limbs whizzed past him. He crawled on one, but the wind overturned the debris, sending him back into the water.

He hissed at the storm; rain pelted him in the face. A log smashed him in the head, causing him to lose his grip on the barter pouch. It slipped out of his paw and began to float downstream, still attached to the log.

"What!" eSmith's eyes doubled in size. He swam after the leather pouch. Paddling faster and faster, he chased after the log; it raced away from him. There had to be a way to get

27

ahead of it, but how? The river often doubled back on itself, instead of a straight run. If he cut across land, he should be able to get ahead of the debris and retrieve the loot.

eSmith dove off the log he had been riding and landed in another messy load of debris. It shifted and wobbled under his paws, but he managed to stay afloat. From there, he made the riverbank and cut across country. The wind whipped bushes and downed trees in his path, but eSmith sped on through the patch of woodland, arriving back at the river.

Hurrying along, he worked his way upriver until he found a huge mimosa. Its long limbs extended in every direction. Several of its limbs were in the river. White water rushed over those sections of the mimosa. That would be the ideal location to spy for the gems, he decided. The limb could hold his weight. He scampered up into the mimosa.

Crawling out on the limb, he waited, his pointy muzzle in the wind.

It did not take him long to locate the leather pouch, still tangled in the pile of debris speeding down river. He adjusted his position, confident that timing was critical to make it work. The debris rushed at him. Water splashed him in the eye.

As the debris rushed past, he dropped down to the lowest limb and extended his paw. A fine mist speared his face as the river's white caps brushed against his paw. He held there, claws sunk deep into the mimosa, suspended in midair. The debris rolled past him.

He latched onto the leather pouch and was nearly pulled back into the river. Struggling with the added weight of the storm, he eventually pulled himself and the wet leather pouch out of the river. He scaled the mimosa limb to the riverbank and moved inland. He could tell there were still loot inside, but he feared many of the precious trinkets had been lost in the river.

He checked inside, pawing over the winnings. Even Zeke's were still there. To his delight, the loot appeared to be all there.

"Yahoo!" He cried in the storm; rain pelted his face as he ran.

Later in the night, he found shelter and slept dry.

***

That evening when the moon stood over the mountains, eSmith heard rattling among the vines and bushes. The storm had left some time back. Yet, the forest and meadows remained damp. He saw no reason to leave. There was no way Brutus and the posse could track him after this storm. He felt confident on that, snoozing well on the idea.

Bushes on the hillside rattled. He saw two pairs of blue eyes glowing in the dark. Hair stood up on his spine, and his right paw began to tingle. They were after him again. Why? When he had grabbed the diamond, every blue-eyed raccoon saw him. And he could see them looking at him too. Talk about freaky. Perhaps they were still connected in some way?

Ears piqued, the gray fox heard the creatures chanting, "Blue, blue, blue."

The blue-eyed raccoons descended the rocky hillside. They tossed aside smaller stones, scrapping claws on the boulders as they approached him, humming, "Blue, blue, blue."

He backed up, seeking a way out. Most of the land about him dropped off back towards the river basin area. West of that led to the plains. Off to his south, a series of canyons and plateaus blocked his path.

He moved in that direction with the crazy creatures in pursuit. He found himself backed against a cliff. It had a twenty-meter drop-off into a narrow ravine.

Two raccoons jumped him, their blue eyes glowing intently. He whirled about and slung the one off his back into the other attacker. They both tumbled off the side of the cliff into the ravine below.

More raccoons attacked; eSmith drove one of them back onto the others. He wrapped an arm hold about the crazy animal's neck. The possessed raccoon twisted and struggled, squealing at the top of its lungs. He shoved the raccoon off the cliff into a narrow ravine to where the others were trapped.

The crazy raccoon bounced off the walls and landed at the bottom with a painful squawk. He jumped up and tried to climb out the ravine, along with the others. They barked madly at him, jumping over each other, trying to scale the steep walls.

"Why are you following me?" eSmith howled down at them.

The possessed creatures kept humming, "Blue, blue, blue."

"What kind of grudge you got against me? I don't have that diamond," he argued.

The crazed creatures did not respond; instead, they kept humming, "Blue, blue, blue."

eSmith backed away. What could he do? He turned and fled, fast as his legs could carry him. They were too freaky. He dashed along the path, darting from rock to tree, hoping the rain would help. The further away he got from them, the better he felt.

***

The gray fox traveled all morning before seeking shelter during the hottest part of the day. Somewhere along the line, he grew tired. eSmith crawled up under an elderberry bush still in bloom. The cream-colored flowers hid him well, even though spring was gone. What better way to pick up a quick meal?

Soon, he grew bored, and sleep consumed him.

At first, only a misty fog smothered him, concealing the world. He could see the foxy fox with the crystal blue eyes and the small underbite. Roxie danced away from him, lost in the mist. He chased after her, only to have Zeke erupt from the fog wielding an ax. The brown and gray wolf tried to chop him in half. eSmith darted to the left to avoid the ax blade, then to the right. Each time, Zeke cleaved off his escape route. The wolf grinned as he raised the ax to chop off eSmith's head; eSmith kicked him between the legs. Zeke gave out a great howl and ran off into the fog.

"You have a bag of tricks," his Uncle Jack howled in the mist. "Use t-h-e-m!"

A silver-haired man boasted, "We can make a fortune on eggs." The big bad wolf hissed from the bushes, "You're behind bars now." The fog parted, for two dwarfs with spears running at him. The dwarves were hot on their trail. They ran blindly into the foggy forest.

When the fog parted, they were alone enough to divide the loot. The big dog had all the gems and eggs while he had one eyeball and two furry sleeping bundles. One of them was a ticking bomb. That did not seem fair, he whined as the ground trembled beneath his paws. Suddenly, a one-eyed giant erupted from the fog, stepping down with a foot twice his normal size. The cyclops crushed everything, including Brubarker and himself.

The gray fox jumped up and howled, "no!"

Sweat peppered his brow. eSmith sat back down. He wiped off the sweat. It had been a dream. That's all it was, a bad dream! Yet, it had been so real at times. Since he could not go back to sleep, eSmith walked until day revealed itself.

CHAPTER FOUR

SNAKE EYE

e Smith had been traveling alone for some time when he took a break on a hill near a bubbling spring. Scouting out the little brook, he crept to the edge of the water. He drank deep and rested his aching back. The bundle with the winnings was taking its toll on his neck and shoulder. He massaged his neck until he heard a banjo singing in the wind. Its melody drew him along a creek into a knoll of thick pines. Emerging into a meadow, the gray fox paused. Fluttering flags and banners drew his attention: a traveling show.

Since getting swept away by the river nearly a moon ago, eSmith had not seen Brutus or the posse. He breathed a sigh of relief that he had finally lost them. He studied the many wagons with the colorful banners flapping in the wind, from a hill overlooking the traveling show.

Strange and wondrous sounds drew the gray fox closer. He had to check them out. There were nearly thirty wagons of various sizes and shapes. Most of them were pulled by mules or horses. Several side shows drew his attention. He wondered if the traveling show was legit.

eSmith looked from his poker winnings to the traveling show and sensed something wrong. He needed to check them out first. He snuck into several wagons, careful not to be discovered. Most of the wagons held the usual stuff: food, clothing, tools, and such. That did not tell him much until he entered the Bearded Hippo's tent and found the large purple velvet pouch with yellow drawstrings. He untangled the drawstrings and opened the pouch. A light brown powder filled it. He took a sniff. Not smelling anything, he sniffed harder. His eyes shot open, and his face erupted in pain. eSmith dropped the pouch and fell backwards against a bearded hippopotamus. His numb nose tingled. He had yet to answer that one.

"Funny little sneak. What are you doing?" growled the breaded hippo. She took several sniffs of the powder and sneezed to clear the airways.

"Ah, that's better." She tied back the yellow strings and returned the powder pouch to the cabinet. "You should not mess with other folks' snuff."

"I didn't know," barked eSmith, rubbing his numb nose. "I can't smell anything."

"Serves you right." She tossed him out of her tent.

eSmith rolled over and stood on all fours. Sniffling about, he still could not smell anything. He drew back for some time and observed. Others came and went without hindrance. He decided it was worth the risk. Now more curious than ever, he moved into the main enclosure of wagons. Several badgers rushed up and tried to sell him some peyote, but he declined.

"Come right in?" shouted a palm reader, waving open the tent. "Learn your fate."

eSmith kept walking. Why would anyone want to know their fate? Wasn't it obvious? Everyone knows they all die in the end.

Many folks stood near the main stage; a red-furred weasel, wearing a blue three-piece suit and a top hat, danced across the platform between two of the wagons.

He grappled with his winnings. They still held a hefty weight and put a crick in his back. His eyes settled on the caravan stage show. He rubbed his numb nose and headed over there. A crowd of spectators had already crowded the stage.

"Welcome one and all to the greatest show in Fairytale Land," the red-furred weasel whistled through a bullhorn, "The main event shall begin shortly. I will be your host. Let me introduce myself. I am Dr. Stouts." He bowed to the crowd; a few clapped back.

"First, let me welcome all those who are suffering from ailments," barked the red weasel. He moved away from the podium to show the crowd his bottle of medicine. The label on the small dark blue bottle read: *Dr. Stout's Tonic and Ailment Cure.*

"Bought the recipe off an old Mesca Medicine Mole. It is all-natural and works wonders. When I begin to ail, I take this cure, and it works. I brew each batch personally to ensure potency. Take one swig every morning, noon, and night before bed. I guarantee it. A spoonful of this elixir every day keeps me young and strong," argued Dr. Stouts.

The crowd mumbled among itself.

"My magical elixir is guaranteed to cure all ailments, or I will personally return your barter," vowed the weasel. He held out the little blue bottle. "Buy three bottles for the price of two. Get it now!"

A few in the crowd forked over a small gem or gold nugget, but most of them could not afford the elixir and could only watch. eSmith clutched tight his winnings, no sense in giving away good barter. He clapped and cheered with the crowd to show his support.

"Thank you one and all for your support. Now we have the fierce hippo warrior queen from the Dark Continent. Please give our fierce warrior a hearty welcome, Queen Hippos, the Bearded Hippo!" announced Dr. Stouts. He bowed and stepped off stage.

The crowd clapped loudly and cheered her on.

eSmith ducked behind others, hoping she would not recognize him. He tried to play as dumb as his nose felt, still unable to smell anything.

Stepping up, the bearded gray hippopotamus mounted the stage. The wooden platform groaned against her weight. The fierce warrior held up a raw iron railroad spike. She passed it around. Several in the crowd tried to bend the spike, but they could not. Once the railroad spike was back in her clutches, she bent it like clay. Dropping it onto the stage, she bowed. Several bystanders failed to unbend the railroad spike. Next, the Bearded Hippo chopped several logs in half in one swipe.

eSmith clapped and cheered with the crowd.

"Wonderful performance," praised Dr. Stouts. "A round of applause, everyone."

The crowd burst into claps and cheers again.

"Thank you. The Bearded Hippo will return during our main event later. Now. from the Orient, we have the Amazing Miniature Pandas."

Six small black and white-furred pandas tumbled onto the stage. The tallest one was no more than half a meter tall. They bowed to the audience. Several crawled onto the backs of the other pandas and backflipped off. They landed in grand fashion.

The crowd cheered. Pandas danced about the platform while others tumbled and flipped, ending with a series of spectacular summersaults to amuse the crowd. They ended by firing a cannon packed with one of them. When they fired the cannon, it projected the panda through the air. The panda cannonball was captured in a net being held by his friends located across the clearing.

The crowd applauded the small black and white-furred bears.

Sniffling loudly, eSmith smelled nothing. He felt his

pointy muzzle. It even felt numb! That snuff was something to avoid.

"More of these amazing pandas' feats will be displayed in our main event later this evening. It will be a glorious event. Now, we have the third and final feat. It pleases me to introduce from New London, Stanton the Sword Swallower."

A whiteish brown coyote appeared on the side stage. A young, rusty-tan vixen danced about. They bowed to the audience.

The foxy fox assistant danced about the coyote, waving a sword. The sword was passed among the attendees to show that it was real.

eSmith checked the blade. It cut him slightly. It brought a drop of blood from his paw. He sniffed at it too, but could not smell anything.

His assistant returned the sword.

The coyote showed everyone the sword. He upended it and shoved the sword, tip first, down his throat. Swallowing the sword, he turned so all could view it.

The crowd gasped and cheered; the coyote slowly pulled out the sword.

Everyone clapped louder while Stanton bowed, departing with his aide.

"There are many more such feats in our main show. It will be starting shortly over in the main tent," announced Dr. Stouts. He tap-danced across the stage. "Don't be late. There will be many spectacle wonders for the eyes. We have the McSquirrels High Flying Acrobats, capable of acrobatic feats sure to amaze anyone. And a singing fox trio sure to warm everyone's heart. Enter and enjoy feats of worth. To the left and the right. We're open most of the night!"

The weasel finished his dance with a plea. "And don't forget my miracle elixir. Watch all your ailments melt away for only one silver ingot."

Getting no takers, Dr. Stouts bowed to the crowd and departed; the crowd dispersed, some heading for the main tent, others mingled among the various wagons.

After lounging about a bit and watching a few small acts, eSmith decided to attend the main event. He paid in a small sapphire and received a free mug of beer. Even though it tasted bitter, free was good.

Beer in paw, he entered the main tent. The enclosure was two levels high, a place to fly and a place to hide from the rain. He took a seat near the front; other folks were scattered about. Suddenly, he yearned for a batch of fried chicken gristle, but no one sold any. There was nothing worse than craving something and having no way of getting a paw's hold on it. He settled on a slab of fresh fried pork skin, lightly salted.

He picked a good spot and squatted down in front of the stage. Chugging on his beer, he chewed on the crispy fried snack. He barely took his eye off the pork skin as the red weasel in the blue suit and top hat danced across the stage.

"Welcome to Dr. Stouts' Traveling Show's Main Event. A spectacular extravaganza for all." The red weasel called out his first wonder, The Panda Troops. The six miniature pandas danced and tumbled across the stage. They did more acrobatic feats, which dazed eSmith.

"Next, we have the famous 'Pin Cushion,' proclaimed the blue-suited weasel.

A mauler treaded on stage. The Pin Cushion was a humongous black bear who could be poked with a variety of items. His assistant poked and prodded him with swords, spikes, spears, and other sharp objects. The sight left many of the audience gasping.

The Pin Cushion ended his act by lying on a bed of nails while his assistant danced on top of him, singing about honey and bees.

While everyone was clapping, the bear and his assistant bowed to them.

"Thank you." Dr. Stouts announced. "And now, for the next event we have a monster. That's right, a freak of nature. Here is Bullanboar the Mighty."

Two cargo handlers dragged a creature in chains and shackles on stage. The minotaur had tusks and horns. The offspring of a bull and a wild boar, he was a mountain of muscle and could lift heavy things easily, such as a travel wagon and large boulders. The beast pounded his chest and bellowed, "I am Bullanboar the Mighty!"

The minotaur pulled apart the chains enslaving him, and removed the shackles. He dropped the chains and shackles on stage then flexed his biceps.

Folks gasped at his escape and moved back, bumping into eSmith, who had already placed them between him and the minotaur.

"It's all part of the show," cried Dr. Stouts.

The crowd settled down as he moved closer to the stage.

Next, the minotaur bent several thick iron bars as if they were saltwater taffy. Dropping the twisted metal bars on the stage, he offered them to the audience for all to check.

"I'll give anyone here a bottle of my elixir who can straighten any of these," shouted Dr. Stouts. He held up his little blue bottle. "Any takers!"

"Me!" shouted a lumber-jackal with red hair and a full beard. Grabbing one of the iron bars, he struggled to unbend it, but he could not.

After several more muscle-bound folk failed attempts to straighten out the twisted iron bars, everyone cheered, including eSmith.

"A round of applause for Bullanboar," shouted the red weasel. "Next, we have our main event. A trio of singing delight. Straight from Nottingham Forest arrives a most exquisite foxy fox singing group. Let me introduce the Magnificent Foxy Trio."

Three young vixens dressed in red and yellow silks danced on stage. They sang a variety of songs which had eSmith humming along. He eyed them intently, comparing them to Roxie, hardly noticing nightfall and the rise of the moon. Candles were lit. The crowd seemed to melt away the more eSmith drank the ale. He tried to forget her by focusing on the three vixens and his numb nose.

He had watched the previous events with little wonder, but once the Foxy Trio performed, he hung on their every word. Lounging in his chair, he grabbed for them as they danced past him. He sniffed at them but could not smell them.

The three foxy foxes slapped his paws aside while performing their songs. Dropping several small rubies in their greedy little paws, he drooled over them. They were so kind.

"Attended a special viewing tonight," announced Dr. Stouts. He told them on the way out. "A round of applause for the Foxy Trio."

eSmith jumped up, howling at the crescent moon.

The trio bowed to the crowd and danced off stage. The three vixens snickered. eSmith paid little attention to the return of the bearded hippo next, his thoughts on the foxy foxes. He hissed if only he could forget Roxie!

"Don't forget. This yummy trio will have a special event later tonight. Now, I want to introduce our next feat of wonder. Let me introduce the Magnificent McSquirrels. Two flying squirrels appeared on stage. They flew into the air, somersaulting off each other.

He hardly noticed the flying squirrels, his mind still on the foxy trio and the event scheduled later that evening. In fact, he thought about little else throughout the remaining show.

Once he left the tent, eSmith went in search of a meal and drink. He found both at the barbeque cart that also served cold beer. Several jackals were having a bad time and were forced to leave by the manager.

eSmith finished his meal and returned for the evening show. He sat up front and drank several brews before the foxy foxes appeared. Padding paws with a few trinkets, he moved closer to the stage to watch them.

"Now, for a very special One Night Only Appearance of the Magnificent Foxy Trio," Dr. Stout chanted. He tap-danced across the wooden floor, shuffling his hips. He bowed to the three foxes before he danced off stage.

The Foxy Trio danced across the planked stage. The nearly quarter moon highlighted them on mid-stage as a long brown snake slithered forward.

"It is my pleasure to introduce Salem, the Fire Serpent. He is renowned for his abilities to swallow fiery swords and hypnotize his audience." Dr. Stouts danced off stage again.

While Salem swallowed several flaming swords, the foxy foxes danced and sang a lively tune. He gently pawed at them. Gigging, the trio ended their melody by draping silk scarves in his face. eSmith licked at them with his tongue.

The snake hung before eSmith, swaying back and forth, hypnotizing him and the crowd. The snake's right eye glowed brighter than his left. How odd, thought the gray fox. He followed the swaying snake, seeing only one snake eye.

Salem slithered across the stage, closing in on the gray fox. The serpent hissed, "Salem says: pay the foxes-s."

"Y-e-s-s," eSmith moaned. He drooled over the foxy trio and dropped several more rubies in their greedy little paws, their eyes glowing like the snake's eyes. Sniffing them, he still could not scent them. He guzzled down more brew, following their every move.

"That pouch-s is-s heavy," hissed the snake. "Free-s yourself of the burden and leave-s now. Never remember this-s night. Remember this-s night never happened-s-s."

"Yes, master!" he barked; eyes unblinking, he wobbled to stand up.

The snake slithered up to the gray fox and removed the winnings.

The Foxy Trio danced about eSmith as he weaved and wobbled toward the exit. They giggled and hissed with delight while they swirled about him.

He stood still, entranced by their performance and those glowing serpent's eyes. They seemed to call him away, far away. The rest of the crowd had also fallen under the snake's spell.

"You-s will remember none of this-s," hissed the snake, eyes glowing.

Everyone focused on the snake.

"I-s will remember none of this-s," howled eSmith with the rest of the crowd. Still motionless, the crowd did not blink.

"Now, go!" Salem, the serpent slithered away with the loot.

"I go!" the gray fox turned about and marched out of camp.

The Foxy Trio laughed at the departing gray fox. They danced alongside him and the others as they marched out of the camp into the night.

CHAPTER FIVE

EYE OUT

The next day, eSmith moved along the mountainous path. He had scented a dwarf rabbit and dove into the bushes after it. The brown bunny hopped over him. He ran into a maple tree and nearly had his right eye poked out. Whirling about, the gray fox shook his head and blinked several times to clear his vision. He chased the short-legged furball a good way before giving up. He sniffed about for more prey but had no success in the hunt.

His thoughts turned toward the Predator's Tavern, and he craved a cold beer with a round of billiards. Everything seemed vague. If only he had some barter. Perhaps his old buddy, Brubarker, may have some from their last heist. Was that the one with the blue-eyed raccoons or the old woman? Wait… eSmith's eyes went wide. "My winnings!"

He searched all his pockets to discover no trinkets. What happened? He had the winnings yesterday at the traveling show. Wait, what about the special event last night? The last thing he remembered was the Foxy Fox Trio of singers. That crafty weasel had something to do with it. And there was a snake there too. He had glowing yellow eyes. The snake must have hypnotized him and taken his winnings. It all smelled rotten.

eSmith refused to turn a blind eye to the truth: he had been conned; now he was determined to get back his winnings and get even.

It took the gray fox a day to track down the traveling show. He was not in a good mood when he spotted them near dusk. He moved in under cover of darkness. The caravan had circled for the night. Several fires were going, and folks were just starting their evening meals.

He crept among them, arriving at the lead wagon: Dr. Stouts' medicine wagon. Crawling up the side, he hid among the flags and banners.

On top of the red weasel's travel wagon, he found them. The group had assembled to split up his winnings and any other tricks. Through the skylight, he eyeballed the group huddling in the wagon. They were all there: the weasel, the Foxy Trio, and the snake. They gathered at the table, surrounding the loot piled in the middle.

"We-s got him good-s-s," hissed Salem the Serpent. The snake slid among the cabinets to arrive on top of the small table. He bumped into a diamond and hissed, "I's-s want my s-share now-s-s."

"What an easy group of marks," squealed Dr. Stouts. He raked through the piles of gems.

"Yes, he was a pushover," sang the lead singer of the Foxy Trio. "It would be nice to have a diamond necklace." The other two foxy foxes giggled with her.

"We did well," barked the red weasel. "That's why I called you here. There's been a change in payment."

"What!" the group shouted.

"Divide-s up the s-spoils now-s-s!" hissed the snake.

"No, we keep the loot together until we get further from here," barked Dr. Stouts.

"Why-s-s-s?"

"Local official. They get complaints and they'll investigate," barked the weasel.

The group mumbled among themselves. Salem, the serpent spoke up first.

"Don't make me-s-s wait too long-s-s." He slithered

away into the night.

The Foxy Trio trailed after the snake.

Once the others had left the wagon, the gray fox crept inside. He found a net meant to trap him and others, but it did not work.

Dr. Stouts shouted to the minotaur, Bullanboar. "I'll be busy inside. Keep an eye out."

Nodding, the muscle-bound bull and boar placed his back to the wagon and crossed his arms. He barred anyone from entering the wagon.

Dr. Stouts scooped up the loot with the flour sack.

"Got you now!" eSmith hissed softly, landing on the table. He grabbed Dr. Stouts by the throat. "Those are mine!"

Breaking loose from his grip, the red weasel darted for the door.

eSmith snorted as he sliced the rope holding the net. He trapped the weasel.

"You're behind this," eSmith barked.

"Help!" shouted Dr. Stouts. He struggled but was unable to escape. He tried to hide the flour sack, but the gray fox caught him.

"That's mine," hissed eSmith. He snatched up the sack, but Bullanboar grabbed his paw and the winnings. He squeezed, crushing eSmith's paw. "Drop the loot!"

"Okay, you win," snarled eSmith. Releasing his grip on the gem pouch, he massaged his paw once the minotaur released him. "Those are mine."

"Property of this traveling show. That's all I know," barked Dr. Stouts. He tucked the loot in his jacket pocket. It bulged out of his jacket.

"You paid that snake to fix me with his eyes," eSmith barked. "Yellow glowing eyes! Or eye? Anyway, you stole my winnings."

"I have no idea what you're talking about," scoffed Dr. Stouts. He straightened his suit.

"Liar!" howled eSmith

Bullanboar grabbed for the gray fox, trying to capture him.

Expecting it, eSmith eluded the minotaur. He jumped on top of the wagon and kicked the back of the minotaur's head.

"Stay out of this!" hissed eSmith; he kicked Bullanboar in the face.

Off balance, the minotaur fell out of the wagon. He hit the ground.

eSmith confronted Dr. Stouts. "You're the thief."

The red weasel hissed at him. "You have no right calling me that."

"I know a skunk in any skin," eSmith barked. He snatched at the weasel's jacket pocket. "I can see it bulging out now, skunk!"

"Really?" inquired Dr. Stouts. He straightened his suit. "Get him!"

Bullanboar rushed the gray fox. But eSmith had heard him coming a long time back. He dove out of the way. The minotaur ran into the tent netting and became tangled in it. The more he struggled to get free, the more entangled he became. Soon Bullanboar could no longer move.

"Ah, there's the rub." eSmith stood over the minotaur.

"How does a fox know Shakespeare?" hissed the red weasel. "Don't taunt me!"

Dr. Stouts ran for the exit, but eSmith was two steps ahead of him. He jumped on top of the weasel, landing with a thump. "Got you now."

"No!" cried Dr. Stouts.

The eSmith pulled the loot from the inside pocket. He weighed the flour sack mentally. They felt about the same. "All my winnings better be here."

"They are," whined the weasel.

Removing several large stones, he held them up, studying them in the light. They made his eye sparkle. Most of the winnings appeared to be there. He returned the gems and gold ingots to the flour sack.

He shoved Doctor Stouts out of the wagon and bowed to the little group gathering outside.

"Come one and all," he announced, "To the greatest scam in Fairytale Land."

The others growled and grumbled at him.

"To be truthful, I feel it was a fair show with mediocre performers. I'm going to rate your show badly. Now get out of my way!" barked eSmith, spotting Brutus. The posse must be near, he considered. The gray fox tucked away the winnings and turned to leave.

Bullanboar charged him.

eSmith side-stepped him, seeing Zeke and Brutus creeping up.

The minotaur rushed past him and hit the wagon. Crashing into it, Bullanboar overturned the wagon. It pinned Zeke and Brutus to the ground.

"Help," howled Zeke. Both his legs were pinned under the wagon. He could not get out.

"Not again," howled Brutus. He whined in pain, tugging on his hind leg. "My leg's never gonna heal."

eSmith landed on the wagon and turned to face them. "Hello?"

They barked and snapped at the gray fox. He jumped off the wagon and dashed away.

The rest of the posse chased after eSmith.

Darting among the wagons and tents, the gray fox wove a path that slowed down the posse. It forced them to backtrack. He eluded them until an idea crossed his mind, and he headed back to the caravan of tents.

eSmith had bought a little time by pinning Brutus and Zeke beneath the wagon. The posse would soon them free, he reasoned. The gray fox paused when he heard from across camp the red weasel bark, "Bullanboar can lift anything."

The creak of the wagon was all eSmith needed to know Zeke and Brutus were now free. He hurried on to the Bearded Hippo's wagon. It appeared dark. Perhaps she was away this time? After the last time, she might not be so easy on him.

eSmith slipped inside the wagon and made quick work of finding it. Checking the cabinets, he discovered the pouch. He held up the large purple velvet pouch and tugged tight the yellow strings. He slipped out the wagon before the Bearded Hippo discovered him. Moving several wagons down, he set the trap to stop Brutus.

"I know he's somewhere around here!" howled the tracker.

"Check every wagon," barked Zeke.

Pulling out the purple velvet pouch by its yellow stringers, eSmith set the trap. He hopped onto another wagon, careful to leave plenty of signs.

Brutus, Zeke, and the posse searched the wagons.

Climbing on the top of one wagon, Brutus found eSmith there, but before he could do anything, the gray fox blew powder in the tracker's face. Brutus inhaled heavily, taking in a good pile of the light brown powder. His face went blank, and his eyes doubled in size.

eSmith darted away.

Pawing at his nose, Brutus howled in disgust. "I'm numb. What happened?"

The tracker rushed about, searching for a way to breathe out of his nose. Giving up, Brutus sniffed loudly and whined, "It hurts!"

"That fox did it," snarled Zeke. "He's sly, that one."

The posse spread out to find the gray fox. Tossing boxes

and crates from the wagons, the group searched the entire traveling show before stopping.

"He's not here!" Chuck announced to eSmith's delight—such sweet revenge!

"I know him well," snarled Brutus. He snuggled down to sleep under a maple tree.

"What're you doing?" Zeke ran about.

"Can't smell. Won't be able to track him until this stuff wears off," barked the brute. "Won't have any idea which way he went until then."

"No!" howled Zeke. Everyone avoided the wolf.

Shouldering the plump flour sack, eSmith made the forest before he stopped. He paused to sniff the air: it smelled clean and free.

CHAPTER SIX

NO EYE LEFT

The rag-tag posse led by Zeke trailed Brutus, who was tracking eSmith. And the predators were hot on the gray fox's trail. He could not distance himself from them. eSmith had tried various tricks to lose them, but Brutus could not be shaken.

The gray fox scrambled up the mountainside, wanting that distance. Far off, an eagle screeched. He climbed up a birch tree to throw them off.

Brutus and the others circled the tree.

"Yeah, I can see him," barked Brutus, shuffling about the tree.

They had him treed until he jumped to a cliff and made the cliff top before slipping away. He crossed the mesa at an alarming rate to end the game, but no plan came to mind.

Near noon, he saw no sign of Brutus, Zeke, or his pack of moguls. He must have lost them for now. eSmith skipped down the trail with his winnings. He caught signs of smoke and trailed it to a campfire near the opening of a cavern.

Sniffing about, he realized it was the home of a Gorx. He had only encountered one of the beasts in his life, and that was with Moxer. They barely got out of that one alive. Gorx were a hybrid of troll and dwarf, and they were known for their solitary nature. When aroused, these beasts became fierce fighters. They have a weird sense of honor, for their word was their bond. They never break their bond.

The Gorx emerged from the cavern, a wide stubby creature. His gray hide bubbled up in places and gave his

52

face a twisted if not demented look.

Hiding behind a maple tree, eSmith barked, "I mean you no harm."

The Gorx grabbed a spear and looked about. Seeing no one, he returned to the campfire where he had plucked several chickens and were roasting them over the flames.

He rotated the birds; the fire hissed and cracked.

The smell made eSmith's stomach growl. Craving the roasting bird, he showed himself to the Gorx and again barked, "I mean you no harm."

Pointing his spear, the beast shouted. "What do you seek here?"

"Food." eSmith stepped closer to the fire. "I'm hungry." The plump and juicy birds made his mouth water.

"I sensed that." grumbled the Gorx; he turned the roasting birds again.

"I've got barter for one of them chickens," eSmith sniffed over the birds, mindful the Gorx had not given his word yet. "Provided you don't eat me."

He dished out a green sapphire and dropped it on the ground before kicking it over to the Gorx; the beast picked up the precious stone and eyed it in the sunlight.

The Gorx snorted at the stone. "More."

"It's good barter," eSmith assured him, careful not to get too close. He tossed over a little red stone. "Here's a ruby too."

"Hum, so be it," the Gorx decided, pocketing both precious stones. "You may select any bird you choose. Eat and go in peace."

Once the Gorx had given his word, eSmith relaxed, for he knew nothing would happen to him while in the beast's camp. Yet, eSmith kept an eye out for betrayal and any new arrivals.

"They will be done soon." The Gorx squatted at the fire and rotated the birds. Standing, he paced back and forth in front of his cavern.

The gray fox squatted near the fire, watching his meal cook. The birds sizzled and popped as they roasted over the flames. *How can humans wait so long?* He drooled over the roasting bird. He craved the aroma more than the roasted chicken.

A silence fell between them. Gorx were known for being fighters, not talkers. He sensed no difference in this one, so he remained silent.

The Gorx removed one of the birds and ate it in two gulps, barely crushing bones with his razor-sharp teeth. He swallowed. The second bird took three gulps and some bone brunching before he licked his greasy gray lips.

Removing his chicken from the fire, eSmith started to sink his teeth into a roasted leg when Brutus hobbled out of the bushes not ten meters away followed by Zeke and the others.

eSmith dropped the roasted chicken on the ground.

The Gorx's eyes shifted from the gray fox to the posse. "Huh."

"There he is!" Zeke howled at the pack. "Don't let him get away."

"Excuse me, but I've got to run," barked eSmith; he took off down the trail.

"Not my fight," growled the Gorx. He picked up the roasted chicken eSmith had dropped and ate it in one gulp, spitting out one of the leg bones.

Zeke and the gang surrounded the Gorx, but the fighter did not seem to notice them. Finally, the gray beast turned to look at the pack before announcing, "This is my camp."

Several in the posse whimpered upon sight of the Gorx's

teeth. Chuck backed up; fear ruled his eyes. "What you think, boss?"

"No problem," whined Zeke, giving the short, stocky gray beast a wide circle. "We don't want no trouble."

The posse also cut a wide path about the Gorx.

"Good. You will live today," snarled the beast, grabbing his spear.

The posse backed up; eSmith ran away.

***

The gray fox stopped on a hill. Far below him the posse was figuring out his trail. Patches of thick fog floated among the dead forest choking the landscape. A faint odor of decay and rot lingered in the air. eSmith gasped for breath, trying to figure a way to lose the pack. He scoffed at a silly idea he just had, quickly dismissing it.

The pack closed in.

eSmith dashed in and out of the rocky terrain. This was not looking good. If he didn't find a way to slow them down, it was over. He would never make the gorge. Touching his winnings, he considered them once more. No, what a foolish thought. Moxer did it once for them to get away. eSmith groaned, for now he understood what the old honey badger meant. Back then, Moxer and him had tried every trick in the book to lose those trackers but could not. It was only when Moxer did the unthinkable that they got away.

There must be some other way, eSmith whined. He searched but could not see any way out of it. The pack would be on him soon, and the winnings would do him no good anyway.

In disbelief, eSmith placed a ruby on the ground. He stood there a moment, wanting to cry before he rushed away. Further up the trail, he placed a silver ingot; next, he set a sapphire at the fork in the path. He left the winnings in places such as in a tree or on a steep cliff or along the edge of a deep ravine or gulch.

Zeke and his pack rushed about, snatching up the winnings. The posse snarled at each other over the loot. Limping along, Brutus sniffed out the trail.

By dropping a gold ingot here, a ruby there, a silver trinket over there, eSmith gave up most of his winnings, but he did slow them down. Soon only a paw-full of the gold, silver, and precious stones remained. The posse ripped apart the empty flour sack in search of any treasure.

"Stop it!" Zeke barked, but the gang continued to argue over the gems.

One of the mutts ran off a cliff after one of the sapphires, falling to his death.

The wolf howled at the pack, "He's distracting us, and it's working!"

One of the other mutts reached for a ruby and fell off the side of a cliff to his death.

"See!" Zeke hissed. He looked over the edge then backed up. He pounced before the pack. "Anything found is mine! Understand?"

"No problem. I'm here for the fox," growled Brutus.

"You heard the boss!" howled Chuck. "All loot goes to him."

The posse mumbled but agreed.

"Now, let's get moving," Zeke snarled at the thugs.

eSmith carefully placed the last of his winnings along the trail, avoiding the dead or dying patches of grass. He paused with a remaining single large diamond in his grasp. At least he would get one thing out of it. Strangely, it reminded him of the blue-eyed raccoons. They too were strange.

eSmith climbed into a cottonwood tree and jumped from branch to branch until he reached a ledge on which to land. He scurried along the narrow ledge, rounding a rocky mound before the pack caught sight of him. The silly idea was the answer after all, he decided.

If there was going to be a showdown, then what better place than Rotter Gorge? It sucked up the greedy as well as the needy. Evil spoke on the wind there. And the rotten stench confirmed it.

Brutus shuffled along, howling, "Get you soon."

He always dreaded going by Rotter's Gorge, but sometimes there was no choice.

***

Rotter's Gorge was not far away now; eSmith headed right for the evil-smelling place. The foul reeking odor of death and decay grew stronger. The stench alone was enough to make most animals throw up. Normally, he avoided Rotter's Gorge too, but this posse hadn't given up and he was tired of running. It was time to end this once and for all.

The vegetation around him struggled to remain green. The trees were little better than dried corn stalks. Many had been strangled by the thorny vines.

He dashed across patches of dead grass. They crunched beneath his paws. It felt weird, so he ran that much faster. Stepping on the thorny vines, he howled in pain. He hot-footed his way along. Whining in pain, he removed the thorny vines tangled about his leg.

Stepping off, eSmith tripped over the vines, and he grabbed for a paw hold.

"No-o-I" he howled as the precious stone slipped from his grip and fell into the evil gorge. eSmith backed up and clawed loose from the thorny vines wrapped about his other legs. The thorns had bitten deep into his leg. He had to rip loose the vines.

The gang spread out to search for his tracks.

"They're persistent," he growled. What he needed to do was to use some of that divide and conquer tactic and turn Brutus against Zeke. That would not be easy, for the brute seemed single-minded. How could he separate Brutus from the posse? Checking his bag of tricks, he found no answer.

So, he led them on a wild chase along the Rose River until he found an answer. A narrow canyon provide the answer. There rested a massive pile-up of boulders and rotting timber near the top of the canyon. The debris was ready to fall into the narrow canyon and block off the path at any moment. He estimated what it would take to make that happen.

He focused his efforts on a large tree resting at the base of the debris pile. A large boulder lodged above it appeared vulnerable. Pushing that boulder down onto the tree could cause the debris to shift and crumble. *It might just work at that!* He decided, hurrying back up the trail. They saw him and came running.

He slid through the small opening, eyeballing the debris that was ready to fall into the narrow canyon. He made it to the other side and waited for the posse to close in before he darted into the narrow passage. He wagged his brush at them.

"We see you," hissed Zeke.

The pack sniffed out the narrow passageway, but they did not enter. Eventually, one of them did enter, but eSmith chased him away by flinging large stones down upon him.

"I don't like the look of this," Zeke barked, backing away from the narrow opening. He smelled a trap. "It stinks."

"I'll do it!" yapped Chuck. He pushed aside some of the thorny vines and crept forward. One of the vines whipped about, slapping him on the rear-end. The thorns bit deep into his hide. He ripped them loose and ran into the back of Brutus. "Ouch!"

Chuck barked and whined, "Sorry!"

"Get out of my way. I'm going," snarled the brute. He pushed aside the bulldog.

Watching the mass of debris, Brutus crouched down and crept into the narrow canyon. He crawled through the opening into the narrow passageway leading to the other side.

Once Brutus made it through the narrow opening,

eSmith pushed on the boulder. It barely moved at first. So, he tried again. It fell away.

The boulder hit the mass of debris above the narrow canyon and started an avalanche of rocks and timber.

Rotten timber and loose stones fell on the tracker. A dust cloud rose in the air. The brute was buried in the rubble. Several of the stones landed on him. A dust cloud settled in the narrow canyon as Brutus struggled to free himself from the debris.

Sneezing, eSmith scouted the debris field. It had worked! The canyon was blocked off from the posse. Brutus pawed the rubble but could not get out. He whined, "Not again."

The gray fox studied the tracker. The brute was trapped under several large slabs of stone. It would be hard to get him loose, but he intended to try. "I mean you no harm."

"Well, I do you," growled the brute.

"I can't keep this hatred alive," barked eSmith. He removed several small stones. Placing his back against one of the larger boulders, he shoved as hard as he could. It barely moved.

eSmith tried to reason with Brutus, "We aren't enemies."

The brute snarled at him; eSmith tossed away more of the stones covering the tracker.

He placed his back against the large slab of stone and pushed again. It moved. Dislodging the large stone, eSmith pulled Brutus free from the rubble, hoping it would help change the tracker's mind.

"Why did you save me?" the brute demanded, rubbing his sore leg. Teeth bared, he stood up and closed in.

"I have nothing against you. It's Zeke I have the problem with," barked eSmith. He backed up to Rotter's Gorge. "He's crazy,"

"He paid me," snarled Brutus. "And I hate you."

"Hate is such a powerful emotion." eSmith dangled a paw towards the evil gorge.

"This is personal *and* business." Brutus jumped at the gray fox.

eSmith pulled back his leg and hopped out of the way of the charging dog.

"No-o-o!" the brute whined, falling into the evil gorge. Brutus hit the soggy ground below. He limped over to the side of the ravine and tried to climb out, but the tracker became entwined in the thorny vines. They dragged him into the bog. Wildly, Brutus pawed for support and cried for help. Rotter's Gorge swallowed him up.

"Goodbye, Brutus. My offer wasn't that bad," yapped eSmith.

***

He heard the baying of Zeke and the posse and hid in a hollowed-out section of a near-dead cottonwood. They must have found a way around the blockade. They were near now, and soon they would catch his scent and be back on his trail.

"They're over there!" Zeke howled to the posse.

The gray fox evaded them by remaining still.

The posse caught his scent and trailed him along the edge of Rotter's Gorge. Another one of the group fell into the evil gulch. The thorny vines strangled the mutt before the dog was sucked under the evil bog. Witnessing the entire scene, Zeke and his remaining posse backed away from the edge of the ravine. "This place is evil."

"He must have fallen in too," barked Chuck.

"Let's get out of here!" barked another one of the mutts.

"Yeah, let's go. We'll deal with that fox later," yapped Zeke.

The others scrambled down the path away from the evil place.

eSmith descended the tree and snorted at their foolishness. He snickered and hissed, "Good riddance."

He hopped and skipped along the rim of the gorge, tap-dancing from rock to tree to the dying grassland to display his joy. He felt like celebrating, so he did.

"Taught you a thing or two," eSmith boasted, clapping his paws together to signify his victory and that he was now ready to wash his paws clean of the whole matter. Turning to leave, eSmith ran into one of the thorny vines. A bolt of pain shot through his head, and he lost vision in his left eye. He felt for his eye. He pealed back the vines until his claws scrapped against several large thorns attached to his eyeball. Removing them meant removing his eye. Then he would have no eye left! eSmith howled in pain; his cries echoed up the gorge.

He heard the far-off baying of Zeke and the crew. They were probably laughing at him, howling in delight at his pain.

eSmith grabbed at his left eye. He backed away and tugged hard to disconnect himself from the thorny vines. A painful bolt of lightning shot through his arms and legs. Darkness consumed him as he fell backwards into the evil gorge.

CHAPTER SEVEN

EYE PATCH

e Smith woke up to a foul stench and a pain in his head. He groaned at the thumping pain on the left side of his head. *My eye!*

"What happened?" He growled, vaguely recalling the thorny vines and losing vision in his eye. He had no vision in his left eye because he had no left eye! Fate had snatched it away. That's why things looked so different. And there was the foul stench, which reminded him of falling in the evil place. That's when he blacked out.

The gray fox rolled over and slid off the ledge. He fell several meters before smashing into a rocky outcropping. Moving back, he nearly became tangled in thorny vines.

Grabbing for support, eSmith struggled to get his bearings. He almost fell off the outcropping again. The next drop was nearly half a kilometer to the swampy ground below, sure death once those vines latched onto him. Backing up, he held on and kicked free of the vines.

He heard the baying of Zeke's friends; they had returned! When they arrived, he backed against the cliff and listened intently to them talking.

"Look. Here's his tracks. He fell over the side," barked one thug.

Zeke yapped, "Her dumping him must have been too much for him."

The posse hissed in delight.

Chuck barked, "Yeah, you see the look on his face when she took off with Charlie?"

The others laughed; eSmith hissed softly. Roxie had picked a mate she desired more. He could not hold that against her, could he? She deserved to be happy, he finally decided, realizing why he was doing it: he still loved her.

"Never liked this cursed place," snarled Zeke. "Let's get back to the tavern."

They departed with chuckles and hisses of delight.

eSmith growled in frustration, struggling to get a firm paw hold. The gray fox stood with his back against the gorge. He moved along the rocky outcropping, looking one-eyed sideways for a way out. Thorny vines crept about him. They grew in every direction. They strangled every tree and shrub encountered. One vine entwined itself about his leg. It began to tighten. He knocked it aside, but other vines kept invading his space.

Why not jump off and end it? He considered the idea for a moment but could not do it. Only a blind idiot would commit suicide. What a fool to end it so quick. There had to be some other way. He moved from one location to the next, looking for signs.

Suddenly, he glimpsed something sparkling ahead. eSmith barely saw it glittering at first, but the more he focused with his right eye, the brighter the light grew. He felt certain it had to be a diamond, but it didn't glitter right. There were flickers of green, yellow, and red. This was no ordinary gem—if it was a gem at all.

He moved closer. Once he struggled loose from the vines crawling up the side of the gorge, the vision cleared in his right eye. And he realized what was sparkling. It was not a diamond, but rather fairies. One of them sparkled more than the others. That fairy had to be a queen, for normal working fairies don't carry dust like that. The enchanting glow about her said it was more than fairy dust. That one had magic involved. The fairies flew about him.

The pain of his missing eye made him snarl. "What do you want?"

"Greetings from our queen!" squeaked one of the fairies.

"I don't care," he hissed at them.

They flew away.

More fairies arrived, zapping this way and that way. It made his eye dance about in his head, trying to keep up with them. They tweeted and hummed, "She is coming! Our mother is coming! The queen is coming!" He winced in pain.

Triumphs blared loudly to announce the queen's arrival. She appeared in a glittering diamond gown and had nearly transparent wings. A crown of gold and diamonds rested on her head. She rode on the crest of a wave of thorny vines along the side of the gorge. The vines surged, raising up the fairy queen enough to view the one-eyed fox for a moment, eye to eye. She gently stepped onto the ledge, and the vines withdrew.

"You appear in dire need," said the fairy queen.

"Save me," eSmith begged her. "My eye."

"We cannot cheat fate. It has chosen you to nourish this evil place."

"Hey, wait a minute! I nourished it with my eye," he yelped. "I never agreed to this fate thing."

"Your carelessness has caused your demise," the fairy queen squeaked, hoovering in his face. Closing her eyes, she touched him. "Yet, I sense your end is not here."

"Right, what's the hurry?" eSmith howled, rumbling about. He could not locate his bag of tricks. The loss of his eye was distracting to him. He failed to locate a solution to finding his tricks or the bag itself because they were probably hiding in it.

"A curse has been placed upon this place." The fairy queen buzzed in his ear. "It'll take much good to counter its evil. You're not worthy of such a task."

"Task? Like what?" eSmith barked, clinging to the side of the gorge. The vines were pulling him down toward the boggy ground below. "I'm listening."

"You're a funny gray one. I don't have time for jokesters." The fairy fluttered away.

"No jokes here," eSmith stood up. "I'm your fox. Whatever you need."

The fairy queen flapped her wings and hoovered centimeters from eSmith's face. She fluttered about him a moment then landed nearby. Sitting down on a rock, the fairy queen crossed her legs and said, "A guardian for the innocent is what I need. It is no easy task. You're not the right candidate."

"Innocent?" eSmith growled at the vines pulling on his leg. "I'm anything you need me to be, innocent or not."

"They deserve better," spoke the fairy queen.

"They who? I got it!" eSmith clutched a firm hold on a tree's roots to keep from being dragged down into the gorge like Brutus. "Please clarify yourselves. All these riddles are giving me a one-eye headache."

"I need a guardian for two orphans."

"What happened to their mother?"

"The evil below has eaten her. Can you raise two predators as your own?" questioned the fairy queen. She fluttered her wings at him, sizing him up.

"I can do it," eSmith promised blindly, clutching for support as the vines wrapped about his leg pulling him closer to the edge. He kicked free of the vines. "You have a deal."

"Huh, I got it! What I'll do is place a spell on you. If you break that vow, a curse will make you lose sight in the other eye."

"What do you mean?"

"Just what I said. You'll be punished if you do not fulfill your task of raising the two puppies for one full year. You'll go blind if you neglect or abandon them. You'll go blind like this," the Fairy Queen snapped her fingers.

The vision in eSmith's right eye disappeared, and he was totally blind. He grappled about, not liking the idea.

"I'll do it," barked the gray fox. He felt about for his missing eyeball. The hole in his face felt weird to him. The throbbing pain blinded him. He closed his other eye to ease the pain.

"I am serious," warned the queen, snapping her fingers.

"I understand," replied eSmith. Blinking, he could see again. "What happens if they should die or something?"

The fairies went silent.

"Oh, I see," barked eSmith.

"Don't let anything happen to them. I gave my word to their mother, and I intend to live up to that word."

"Okay," he howled. "You have a deal.

"Very well," said the Fairy Queen. She gave the nod to several of her servants. They flew off in every direction.

Shortly, the fairies floated a rope before him. eSmith latched onto it. He climbed onto the narrow ledge closer to the top of the evil gorge. The thorny vines on the ledge, recoiled from his touch.

A leather pouch landed on the ground at his paws. The fairies opened the pouch, revealing two sleeping puppies. Eyes shut tightly; the puppies slept soundly.

"They're coyote puppies!" eSmith barked. "I'm a fox."

"A puppy is a puppy. And there are two here. You will take care of them, raise them like your own or meet your fate." The fairy queen announced.

"I promise," eSmith vowed. He added. "Can you at least fix my eye?"

"We will not go against our mother's wishes." The fairy queen ruled.

"I've accepted your offer," howled eSmith, losing his hold. He fell towards the gorge. He struggled to get a firm paw hold, head throbbing painfully. He slipped closer to the bog. The smelly weeds reeked of death. He barked as the vines wrapped about his neck and began to choke him. He gasped for air.

The Fairy Queen waved her wand, and the vines receded.

"What about an eye patch?" he yelped, struggling to separate himself from the thorny vines. "Yeah, why bother. I'll probably die from the infection anyway."

The Fairy Queen chuckled at the gray fox. "You are persistent. Very well, you will suffer no infection. This eye patch will help heal the wound, too," declared the fairy queen. She waved her wand, and an eye patch appeared. It hovered in the air.

It reminded eSmith of a pirate's eye patch. It settled over his missing left eye.

"Now adjust the patch to the most comfortable position. There it will remain," promised the fairy queen. She waved her magic wand.

eSmith carelessly adjusted the eye patch. It felt a tad off—slightly crooked, and it occasionally itched. Yet, he left it.

"So be it!" She waved her wand, and the eye patch sparkled about the gray fox's head. It settled over his missing left eye.

He tried to remove the eye patch, but he could not. The patch remained there as the fairy queen promised it would. "Good, at least it doesn't hurt. Now what?"

"Now sleep, and when you awaken, you will be out of the gorge," said the fairy queen.

"Don't forget to awaken the puppies, and you must say the word, *awaken*, three times."

"Awaken, three times, I got it. But what if I don't want to sleep," barked eSmith.

"Sleep! Sleep! Sleep!" the fairy queen chanted. She waved her wand over his head.

"Oh, well, I can do with a nap," he yawned.

The Fairy Queen waved her wand. "Good night." She flew away.

Fighting to stay awake, eSmith felt himself floating up to the top of the gorge. He gently landed next to the sleeping puppies. They appeared sweet and innocent. Closing his eye, he felt himself being pulled against time; days rolled past as he drifted into sleep. Lights and flashes of red and blue met his dreams. His world stopped spinning, and he drifted into a deep slumber.

CHAPTER EIGHT

ONE-EYE CRAZY

Awakening, eSmith found himself on top of the gorge in the meadow grass near a spring. The morning sun was low in the sky, and birds chirped happily about him. There was a lot of food, so he ate twice. The leather pouch had been laid at his paws. Looking inside, he found the sleeping puppies. They looked innocent and sweet.

He secured the pouch and started along the trail. He often walked sideways, having to adjust his walking habit due to having only one eye.

His stomach growled one day later and did not stop for another three. He became so hungry it was all he could think about. He searched for a meal under bushes, in trees, and the tall grassy meadows. He rousted a quail, found the nest, and had a decent meal. Belly full, he moved on.

Traveling most of the morning, he stopped for a drink at a stream. He cleaned his wounded eye best he could since he could not remove the eye patch. It itched like it was healing.

He waded across the creek before he realized the pouch holding the puppies was submerged underwater. He held it out of the water until he made the other riverbank. He checked in on the puppies. They were asleep, wet, and shivering inside the leather pouch. He set them on top of the pouch in the sun to dry.

After a nap, he checked the little sleeping ones. They were dry, so he returned them to the leather pouch, and eSmith headed back to the creek. He drank for a long time.

Once he finished quenching his thirst, eSmith hopped off

down the trail, his thoughts on the Predator's Tavern. The vision in his right eye began to blink off and on.

"What's going on?" he pondered, rubbing his eye. Then he remembered the Fairy Queen's warming. What about the pups? He had forgotten them! He had to find them before he went blind permanently.

He rushed back to the place where he had left the leather pouch with the sleeping pups inside. The pouch was gone!

He stumbled about, his eyesight blinking in and out. "I get it!"

Heading east, his eye blinked off; he reversed directions and headed west. He scrambled in that direction as fast as his paws could carry him. This vision in his right eye improved. *Yes, they were this way,* he felt sure. He rushed on, closing in on the pouch. If he had not been so preoccupied, eSmith might have heard the whistling.

A copper brown jackal danced along the trail, skipping while he whistled a lively tune.

"Hey, wait up," howled eSmith. He scrambled over a large rock and slipped on a half-fallen tree, fell to the ground at the jackal's paws. He barked, "Hold on there!"

"Hold who?" snarled the jackal. He turned abruptly and pursued a narrow path along the canyon's rim down to the river. "This is my meal."

"What!" eSmith blinked hard. With his vision diminishing, he had to rush to keep up.

"I'm getting hungry too," grumbled the jackal.

"That's my pouch!" snarled eSmith. He had been through this area a few times and knew it well. Abandoning the trail, he darted along the hillside.

"Finders' keepers, Ma always hissed," the jackal howled.

"I'll give you something else," eSmith promised. The vision in his right eye faded; he ran faster to kept up.

"Losers weepers," hissed the jackal. He trotted on.

"I need that!" howled the gray fox. He hit the ground and saw stars. His vision returned; things grew brighter.

"They're mine!" the jackal snarled, standing over him. "Stop wasting my time."

He took off at a gallop, rushing up the trail.

eSmith's eyesight began to falter as he fell behind the jackal. He rushed to keep pace. He did not like the blind part. Hopping over boulders and into trees, he grabbed for the leather pouch on several different occasions, but he could not secure it.

By this time, the jackal had become paranoid, for the gray fox was near or not far behind. "Go away!"

"Give me that!" howled eSmith, snatching at the leather pouch.

"It's mine!" hissed the jackal, stumbling along the trail. Around the bend on the trail, he bumped into eSmith. He kept trudging along with the pouch.

Nearly falling down the mountainside, eSmith hesitated a moment, fearing the jackal as much as going blind. He kept on the trail leading them into a small meadow near the lake.

"I have barter," whined eSmith.

"You have nothing I want," hissed the jackal. "Now go away!"

eSmith remained close, avoiding the predator. He darted this way and that way.

The jackal tried to elude him, but eSmith kept close. He started south and found the gray fox hiding under a bush. eSmith exploded out of a blooming rose bush, snatching for the pouch, but he missed again. Then the gray fox dropped from a tree like a pine cone, but he still did not acquire the leather pouch.

The jackal turned the opposite direction and headed that way, finding the gray fox concealed in a hollowed-out tree stump. Turning east, he found eSmith crouched in a tree. In the opposite direction, the gray fox stood on a rocky mound waving at him!

The jackal sneered at him. He was twice the size of the gray fox.

"Stop this!" eSmith barked. "I'm tired of chasing you."

"You calling me out?" hissed the Jackal at the one-eyed fox. "I'll eat you alive."

"I'm not all that tasty."

The jackal flexed his muscles and snarled. "You're one eye crazy!"

"Whoa, there's no reason to bad mouth us disabled," snarled eSmith. He rolled over and darted for the jackal. "I need that pouch. My pups are inside."

"Those pups are yours? Liar, I know coyote pups when I see 'em," hissed the jackal. He took off across the meadow, heading for the tree line.

eSmith gasped as darkness consumed his vision. He clutched about in the darkness, hoping to find the jackal. "Give me back that pouch!" he howled at the top of his lungs.

"What's going on here?" growled a deep voice.

"Where have I heard that voice before?" eSmith scratched his head once he caught the bear scent. Now, he was really confused. Wait! There had been a brown bear a long time ago, the one he had helped free from the pit, something to do with fur or Autumn or sun.

"H-e-l-p!" hoarsely choked the jackal.

"Fox is a friend to Fur of Autumn Little Sun," the brown bear roared. He stripped the pouch from the jackal and returned it to the gray fox.

"Thank you," howled eSmith. He could see the light once more. Soon all the vision returned in his right eye. "You have saved my life, Little Sun."

"Yes, I now return the favor," groaned the brown bear. Little Sun released his choke-hold on the jackal. "Go and do not bother my friend no more."

The jackal stumbled off. He howled in disgust and rage, limping away.

"You are most kind, Little Sun," barked the gray fox, checking inside the pouch. The puppies were still sleeping soundly. He breathed a sigh of relief and remarked. "I see you have healed well since last we met."

"Mother heals us all, good friend," rejoiced Little Sun. He ripped open a log and snacked on a pile of termites.

"Yes, my friend. She heals us all," eSmith barked, wanting a way out without having to wake up the two puppies. There just had to be a way, and he was determined to find it.

CHAPTER NINE

EYE WIDE OPEN

e Smith clutched tight the leather pouch holding the puppies. Now that he had the pouch back, he felt no need to rush in waking them up. He thought of the foxy fox, Roxie.. She was gone. The one with the icy blue eyes and silky red brush with the gold tip had chosen another. A single tear rolled down his right cheek; he sobbed in the wind. "She betrayed me. Left a hole in my heart."

The gray fox worked on the bottle of liquor he had bartered off a moonshiner. The liquor made it easier to forget her until hunger set in, reminding him the real world still waited and the coyote puppies he had vowed to raise.

He totted the leather pouch for some time. The leather strap cut deep into his shoulder; eSmith massaged his shoulder before checking on the puppies. They were still sleeping. They appeared so sweet and innocent. He lingered over the idea of waking them up. The only thing to do was say the word "awake" three times. One day, he decided. They must stay that way until he got them a meal. Yes, he must have a meal laid out as the fairies had done for him. Perhaps that was their intention all along?

His stomach grumbled again.

Starting back towards Fairytale Village, he picked up the dog sign. He smelled the paw scent; instantly, he knew it was Brubarker. His old friend was not far away. Hurrying along the trail, he searched for any cut-away sign. The Misfit never varied on his journey. Soon, the gray fox heard the big dog's paws slapping the ground, and then his friend ran into view.

The big dog galloped down the trail like a steed, tail raised high, almost like he didn't have a care in the world.

eSmith quickly caught up, barking. "What's up, Misfit?"

"Huh?" the big dog sniffed about. "Where have you been?"

"What do you mean?"

"It's been nearly two moons since we last talked."

"Two moons! I've been gone that long?" eSmith tried to reason it out. Was it possible he had slept that long? eSmith scratched his chin. The fairies did it somehow.

What had he been doing for two moons? He had no idea. Perhaps he had slept the whole time. So that's why he had been so hungry when he first woke up.

"Yeah," barked Brubarker. "What happened to your eye?"

"I got jumped by two bobcats who I owed barter," fibbed eSmith. "One of them nearly snatched out my eye."

"Told you about that crowd at the tavern," yelped Brubarker. "They're a rough lot. Hey, what do you mean by nearly?"

"Well, anyway, while running away from them crazy cats, I ran into a unicorn."

"A unicorn?" barked the Misfit.

"Yes, a unicorn and the wizard riding him told me to keep an eye open," the gray fox barked, shouldering the leather pouch.

"Really?" Brubarker considered.

"Of course, it's the absolute truth. Sort of," eSmith slyly grinned, scratching his eye patch. "What about you?"

"I'm working steadily over at the mill. My lady's running that orphanage now and wants me to settle in," yapped Brubarker. "Settling down is good for some of us."

"I can understand that," barked eSmith. He touched his missing eye, thinking of Roxie.

"Really?" inquired the big dog.

eSmith told him about losing Roxie. He barked, "The hate transformed me into a compassionless monster like the humans. I didn't even realize it. I've got my eye wide open to things now. You can bet on it." He adjusted the strap on the leather pouch.

"Good," panted the big dog. He scratched his head. "What'd you got there?"

"Kin," eSmith yelped, opening the pouch to show the sleeping coyote puppies.

"Whose pups are those?"

"They're mine."

"Yours? Huh?" the big dog growled.

eSmith nodded, "Mine now. I've got to raise them."

"They've been sleeping the whole time?" Brubarker inquired, scratching an ear.

"Yeah," barked the gray fox. "Kind of forgot about them."

The Misfit sniffed over the puppies, but they did not wake up. He barked, "What's wrong with them?"

eSmith explained what happened, ending with, "They're under a sleeping spell. When I say awake three times, they're going to wake up. And they won't stop barking for food once I wake them up."

"They'll be hungry," the big dog admitted. "Real hungry."

"That's why I'm not in such a hurry," confessed eSmith.

"That's not right," Brubarker yapped. "You couldn't leave them asleep."

eSmith growled at his big friend, "You're right. The fairies are making me do it."

"Kits aren't all that bad," the Misfit barked. "My pups cheer me up a lot. It's nice to have folks to need and care about you. That's what family's all about."

"True, but I'm not ready for this," eSmith barked.

"You'll never be ready," barked the big dog.

Perhaps the Misfit was right, and he never would be ready, but that did not remove his obligations. An idea popped into his mind. "We need a caper. How else am I going to feed them?"

Brubarker lowered his head and growled.

"One last heist," barked eSmith.

The Misfit raised his head and groaned. "Okay. Any ideas?"

"How about a few pheasants?" yapped eSmith

"Haven't had a pheasant in a while," barked Brubarker.

"Thought so," added eSmith. "They're not far away, either."

***

The Tuckers were a dwarven clan who lived a five days march east of Fairytale Village. The dwarves had a large cabin with a lean-to added on the back where their sons lived. Pheasants and pigs ruled the barnyard. Old Tucker's seven sons were spitting images of the old dwarf.

The two burglars rested at the edge of the forest under a dogwood shrub near a stream. The dwarves farmed a few plots of cleared land in the forest. One of old Tucker's sons was always guarding the coops. It had been a long time since eSmith had raided the place.

The dwarves had built it up over time. Both of the bird coops looked better built than before. And now there were three dogs. This would not be so easy. The gray fox stashed the pouch with the puppies high up among the thick branches of a blue spruce. He felt certain they would be safe there. Climbing down, he met up with the Misfit.

The dogs howled at their scent, forcing eSmith and the big dog to withdraw.

"What's going on out here?" A young dwarf appeared with a spear in hand. He scratched his beard and walked about, checking both the chicken coops and his dogs.

The dogs growled from the scent of Brubaker and the gray fox, but eventually, they settled down. eSmith circled the coop and met up with the big dog.

"Can't get in that coop. What now?" whined Brubarker, patting his belly.

"Huh?" eSmith studied the cabin, sensing movement inside, toward the front door. They were the soft patter of small feet. The door opened, and there appeared a middle-aged dwarf. The dwarf wore an apron and held a wood roller in hand. This had to be the mother. . . dwarf?

She tapped on a piece of iron attached to a leather strap. She rang the metal bar. "Supper boys. Get cleaned up."

"Yes, Ma," replied a young dwarf with a strong chin and hazel eyes.

"Norm, get your brothers," she said, heading back into the cabin.

"Yes, Ma." The youngest dwarf headed for the barn.

"I'm hungry too," whined Brubarker.

"Not yet. Soon. . . this might work," eSmith rubbed his chin. Now was the time to get something to eat.

The dwarves arrived, rolled up their sleeves. They washed their arms, hands, and faces. "Ma's got vittles done."

Brubarker growled low; eSmith slapped a paw over the big dog's snout.

eSmith kept the Misfit silent while watching the dwarves enter the cabin. He heard small feet shuffling across the dirt yard. It was a pheasant. He heard another one rush past him.

They crept up to view the family between the slats of the shutters. The dwarf family gathered about a long table. Including the grandparents, there were twelve of them, all various sizes but none over a meter in height. Once prayers were done, they filled their plates and chowed down.

Old Tucker spoke first. "Boys, once you finish eating, put the cow in the barn tonight."

"Sure thing, Pa," agreed the eldest son.

"Ma makes the best pheasant and dumplings I've ever eaten," said the youngest dwarf.

"Ma's buttermilk dumplings are the best," agreed another one of the sons; he wolfed down his food, scooping it into his mouth.

Once the talk died down, the dwarves focused on their meal.

eSmith watched them between a slit in the window shutter from outside. Certain they were busy, eSmith tapped the big dog on the shoulder and backed away.

"Let's go!" he hissed.

They trampled across the yard, avoiding the chicken coop and the dogs. He saw another pheasant dart across the yard and duck into the barn. Perhaps there were enough pheasants to meet the task?

They ran about the barn, searching for a way in, but the door would not open, and the windows were also latched shut. Any cracks in the walls were too narrow for eSmith to slip through. He kept looking for a way in.

"There must be an opening," softly whined the big dog.

"You're right," agreed eSmith. "Keep looking."

They searched the sides of the barn and around the back.

Eventually, they discovered several loose boards. They forced a small opening and went inside. The barn had several stalls on the bottom and a hay-loft up top. There were plenty of hiding places. With the main doors closed, the place was cool and damp, even promising a good sleeping area during the heat of the day.

eSmith snatched up a discarded seed bag. "We've got an egg hunt."

"Egg hunt?" yapped Brubarker.

eSmith located a nest in the corner of the stall, among the hay and dried grass. There were eight small, speckled eggs in the nest. He chewed on one. "Mighty tasty."

"Them little things," growled the big dog.

"Plenty of them birds around here. eSmith showed him another nest full of eggs. He munched on two more.

When the birds caught a whiff of the gray fox's scent, they raised a fuss and dashed away. He found several more nests full of eggs, quickly placing them in the seed sack, along with one pheasant determined to protect her nest.

Brubaker dashed about the barn, snatching up any pheasant who happened to block his path. "I'm so hungry," The Misfit wolfed down a bird on the spot.

***

Once they cleared the barn of all the pheasant eggs and any unfortunate birds, the two burglars returned to the backside of the cabin. They sniffed about and found more eggs.

eSmith froze in his tracks; he dropped the seed sack. His mouth fell open, drooling. A steaming pile of pheasant gristle blocked his path. It smelled fresh, sweet; he tasted a bit of buttermilk dumplings. Attacking the steaming pile of bones, he gobbled them up.

The big dog wolfed down some of the bones too. Ears piqued, he choked on one of them. He could not breathe, face turning red. Brubarker wheezed and coughed until eSmith jumped on his back and the bone popped out.

eSmith snacked on the last few bones.

The back door to the cabin opened, and the mother-dwarf carried out more table scraps. She stopped on the back porch in sight of him. She froze there a moment then screamed. "Fox! We got a fox!" The dogs started barking madly.

Dropping the pheasant bones, eSmith grabbed the seed bag. He ran for the forest, but the bag weighed him down. He dumped the bag in front of the Misfit. "Help!"

Brubaker grabbed the sack in his teeth and followed. eSmith quickly retrieved from the blue spruce the pouch with the puppies. Checking inside, he found them soundly sleeping.

Slinging the pouch cross-shoulder, he barked. "Let's go."

"About time," barked the big dog.

They made the woods long before the dwarves could pursue them. They ran for some time before looking back to see if they were still being followed.

The Tuckers pursued them deep into the forest before they entered a clearing where birds circled overhead. Eagles screeched high above them.

When the Tuckers looked up, the eagles had already struck. Two eagles snatched up the youngest dwarf. The birds struggled to gain altitude.

"Help!" cried Norm. He tried to get free, but one of the eagles knocked him over the head with a talon. He went limp.

"Stop!" shouted one of his brothers. He threw his spear at the birds but missed.

Several other Tuckers tossed their spears at the birds, but all fell short.

The bird gained altitude, nearing the cliff where eSmith and Brubarker hid.

"Oh Lord, help my son!" shouted old Tucker. Tears slid down the old dwarf face as he watched his youngest son being carried away by two eagles, and he was helpless to stop it.

eSmith had also watched the eagles carry away the old dwarf's son. Old Tucker cried as his sons dashed about, unsure of what to do. A sliver of guilt crept into eSmith's being. He pondered why he felt such guilt: the puppies, perhaps?

"We should do something," grumbled the big dog.

"Thinking the same thing," yelped eSmith. His good eye settled on a spruce sapling. *Now that might just work,* he considered. He barked, "Quick, bend over that sapling."

The big dog landed on the young spruce and bent it over.

eSmith placed a paw-full of the eggs on the branches. Focusing on the eagles, he lined the small eggs up with his pointy muzzle then barked, "Now!"

The big dog released the tree; it sprang up, and the eggs went flying. One of the eggs hit an eagle in the head, stunning the bird. He dropped his end of the dwarf.

Norm fell to the ground. He hit with a solid thump. Rolling over, the young dwarf stood up and shook his fist at the eagles.

"You're saved!" cried the old dwarf.

eSmith saw thanks glitter in Old Tucker's eyes. Perhaps compassion can be learned, after all, he mused.

The old dwarf and his sons gave up the hunt and returned home.

***

The gray fox and the Misfit rested under a cottonwood near a stream. There, among the short grass along the bank, they revealed the loot. They had a bag full of eggs and pheasants.

Many of the eggs had survived. He could not count all of them. And there were at least eight plump pheasants too. It was going to be one grand feast!

eSmith divided up the loot with Brubarker. They feasted again on more pheasant eggs and had a good nap. He did not want to think about what he needed to do next.

Waking later in the day, eSmith stood up and stretched. "You're going home?"

"Yeah," Brubarker stretched too. "Change your mind again?"

"No," hissed eSmith, starting to leave, he picked up the leather pouch. He weighed the two coyote puppies and looked inside. They were still sleeping.

"Are you still going to lug that thing around?" yapped the big dog. "Be brave."

"Okay," eSmith conceded. "I'm going to wake them up."

"Good for you. It takes guts to raise a family," Brubarker growled. "Love is as powerful a force as hate."

"Who told you that?"

Tail sticking up in the air, the big dog stood tall and proudly proclaimed. "My Momma."

eSmith stood tall too, but not that proud. He reached for the pouch.

"Well, here we go." He pulled out the coyote puppies and placed them on the ground.

"Wake up, wake up, wake up." He finished the chant.

The puppies did not stir.

"What's wrong?" barked Brubarker.

eSmith scratched behind his right ear with a hind paw while he considered the problem. "I could have sworn she said three times, the word, wake, or was it--awaken, awaken, awaken."

The puppies yawned and slowly opened their eyes.

"It worked!" he howled in delight, picking them up. They stretched out then licked his face. Perhaps he didn't need a foxy fox after all.

"Stop that!" eSmith scowled, but they licked his face anyway. One of the coyote puppies had a brushy brow and determined eyes, while the other had a tongue sticking out, pointing upward. He snickered. "You two are cute."

"That's why we love them so much," barked the big dog. "They grow on you."

eSmith ushered the little ones to the pheasants and eggs. "Eat well."

"Have you named them yet?" inquired Brubarker.

"Never thought of names," yapped eSmith.

"Well, you should," the big dog assured him. "You're their father."

"Me? A father?" eSmith marveled at the idea.

The two kits howled at the feast. They jumped into the meal.

The gray fox glared at them. "Don't you think I need to know them first?"

"No," woofed Brubarker. "Just don't be coy about it."

"Coy? Hadn't thought of them in a long time," eSmith reflected on his long-gone sisters, Koy and Kay, while the puppies played tug-a-war with a pheasant. "Being coy is a family thing."

THE WOLF AND THE CALLOUS CHILD

By
GranRan

Lebo Wolf heard them long before he saw the boy, the dog, and the mule. The gray and black wolf crouched in the bushes and waited on the cart path as he had often done for a free meal. There's nothing like having your meal delivered. He sniffed them out. The child was around eight-years-old and slumped over slightly when he walked. He had cruel brown eyes and a small scar crept across his right temple. A young puppy ran at the boy's heels.

The brownish tan puppy, a mix of hound and bulldog, tagged along, ears flopping up and down as he kept stride with the whinny donkey that pulled a wood sleigh.

The cunning wolf watched them from the bushes. They made enough noise to wake every forest demon in the area, Lebo mused. He keenly observed his prey for he did not want to lose a meal before getting the chance to sample it.

Mostly it was the boy who made the noise. He stumbled through the underbrush like a blind stag. The child had no idea how precarious his situation had become now that he was out of sight of the other villagers. Many folks have entered the Forbidden Forest and many have never left it. They were swallowed up by the forest or something. There were things that happened un-naturally in there that even terrified him. Things that upset the natural order and left a nasty taste in the mouth.

The boy drove the mule and wooden sleigh off the path into the dense forest. He reigned over the mule with one hand, and with the other hand slung a whip over the back of the animal.

"Get moving!" the boy shouted.

The mule hee-hawed his protest.

Lebo crept forward.

"Get up there!" shouted the callous child. Flapping the reins, he laid on the whip.

The mule reared back and tried to shake off the blows. He wheezed in pain and dropped his head to plow forward. Trampling the underbrush, the mule bulldozed over a patch of young elms. Several smaller animals broke cover and ran for deeper woods, including a rabbit.

The rabbit ran straight at the gray wolf. Mouth open, Lebo snapped it shut on the rabbit. The hare stopped twitching; he chewed up the rabbit, fur and all.

It barely quenched his hunger. He considered going elsewhere for his next meal, but the hunger returned. Perhaps he could lurk the puppy into the bushes. He pondered how. Call to him? The young dog was not that dumb, was he? He chose a simpler trick.

The lone wolf rustled the bushes, catching the puppy's attention. The puppy didn't take the bait, backing way. He growled low and deep.

Lebo pulled further back into the forest. If he could not get the long-eared puppy then there was the mule. He would not be as easy a prey with those hooves. Either one would make a worthy meal.

The whinny mule settled down to braying his discontentment; the boy lashed him again with the whip. The beast of burden pulled deeper into the thick underbrush.

"Whoa!" shouted the child. He reined in the mule. "This will do."

He shoved the little dog out of his way. "Get! Why are you blocking my path?"

The boy bullied his way into the forest and brought along an ax too. With a malicious look on his face, he slapped the young dog on the nose.

The puppy whined as he backed away, nearing the bushes where Lebo Wolf rested.

The clever wolf crept forward to eat the puppy, but the little dog ran away.

"Now you get the idea," sneered the boy. His cruel eyes held a sour attitude.

Lebo kicked a small stone into the bushes away from his location.

"What was that?" The boy stopped and turned to where he had heard the rustling bushes. His eyes grew wide. He backed up and ran to the sleigh.

Grabbing a spear, the boy pointed it at the forest. His cold calculating eyes studied the underbrush. He poked the nearest bush, spearing anything underbrush. He probed bushes for some time before feeling secure. He leaned on the spear a while then sat down next to the puppy. He slapped the puppy on the head and said, "Bad dog. Since that bear killed Pa, I haven't eaten decent. None of them villagers care."

The long-eared mule hee-hawed.

"Hush up," he snarled. "Heard something out there."

Lebo pulled back, hoping the child had not seen him. The puppy drew close to the boy and growled.

"There's a wolf out there." The puppy growled at the bushes, but the boy did not understand him.

"Heard it too, did you?" The boy braved the bushes, jabbing them with his spear. "Probably a fox or coyote." He kicked the bushed with his feet.

Another rabbit darted between the boy's legs. He jumped back and fell on his rear-end. "Ouch! A dumb rabbit."

The puppy growled at the bushes where Lebo crouched, ready to pounce on them the moment he was discovered.

"It's a rabbit, hush!" shouted the child; he kicked the dog.

Setting aside the spear, the boy grabbed the ax. He hacked limbs off a recent dead fall and began stacking the wood on the sleigh. A few rounds of cutting and stacking brought sweat to his forehead. Wiping it away, the boy swung the ax with a sharp eye. He chopped wood most of the morning until the sun cast shadows directly overhead.

He took a break and drank from a water pouch at the wood sleigh and noticed movement overhead, high in the trees. He reasoned aloud. "Squirrels, I bet."

Wrong again, Lebo snarled deep in his throat.

The child set his water pouch on the sleigh and returned to work.

***

The sun rose high in the sky before Lebo could actually close in. Trees shielded them from most of the day's heat. The boy finished loading up the sleigh. He grabbed the reigns and his whip. He shouted, lashing the mule across the back, "Yah!"

The mule trampled the underbrush, struggling to get a footing. He brayed.

"You can rest when we get out, Yah," barked the callous child. Viciously, he lashed at the mule. He drove the whinny beast forward, forcing the mule to pull the sleigh out of the underbrush towards the trail.

"Get up there! Get moving!" shouted the boy. He applied more whip to the mule's back. It took several lashes to get a response: the mule reared up in his harness, dug in his hind legs and pulled that much harder. The wood cart crept forward. Eventually, the mule pulled the wood sleigh back onto the cart path.

"Whoa," shouted the boy. He left the mule in the sun and sought shade under an elm. He yawned, "Now for a little nap."

Nearly collapsing from the task, the mule trembled under the noonday sun, whimpering through parched lips. The mule dozed in the sun while the boy napped in the shade.

Lebo studied the sleeping child. What a heartless little beast. That boy was a good example of why he could never trust a human. They're that way from birth, he reasoned.

He drew near, keeping down wind. The boy's sweaty odor reeked. In fact, the child stunk, leaving a nasty smell in his nostrils.

Lebo spat out the foul taste. Another reason why he hated dealing with humans. A mule or dog had good meat, but human flesh was tainted unless it happened to be a sweet innocent child. And most children weren't innocent. Most of the time, a child's acts of cruelty and callousness tended to taint their meat. Not only that, but the child's death usually causes an uproar in the village. They'll be latching down shutters for moons. Then the brave men will gather in the village square for the customary "wolf hunt" which will either end in his death or some other poor creature caught in his stead. No, the human was not worth it.

While the boy napped, the puppy ate his food. The puppy finished his Master's meal and went to thank him. He licked the boy's face, startling the child awake.

"What!" shouted the boy upon finding his food eaten. He struck the puppy with a stick several times and yelled, "bad dog!"

The puppy crumbled into a whinnying mess, allowing the callous child to beat him. The boy hit him several more times and kicked the dog in the side. He snarled. "You're a dumb dog."

Lebo grinned sourly. The callous child will beat the puppy to death. All that he needed to do was wait. If there was one thing Lebo had plenty of, that was time. He crouched low and waited. The wolf licked his lips; naive makes a fine meal.

The boy kicked the puppy again. "Stay out of my food."

The dog rolled over, barely able to raise up.

Now was the time. He closed in. The puppy and mule would make a wonderful meal, he considered until he moved in on his real prey. Lebo pounced on the child, disregarding the chaos it would create. He latched onto the boy's throat, having decided to create fear in the village. It would do the villagers good to live in fear's presence once more.

The boy grabbed for his spear and whined for his mother. He made gurgling noises as he struggled to breathe.

Lebo applied more pressure until the boy stopped struggling and went limp.

"Go!" Lebo Wolf hissed at the dog and mule, "Now!"

"Yes, Mister wolf," barked the puppy. Ears flopping, he limped back toward the village.

The mule hee-hawed and took off. Loose bits of wood tumbled off the sleigh as he rushed along the path. The puppy dodged the falling firewood, keeping up with the mule and wood sleigh.

Lebo Wolf feasted until his belly swelled up. Even a callous child makes a good meal on occasions. Eventually, he moved on, leaving the remains for the scavengers. With a good healthy burp, the lone wolf dashed into the forest, never to look back.

THE END

Available in all Major Outlets
Tales of eSmith's early years

The Magical Meniscus
Available in All Major Outlets

GranRan Bio:

GranRan earned a Master in Arts in the sunny state of Carolina in 2007. He enjoys golf, fishing, and camping with the grandchildren. His novella, *"The Magical Meniscus,"* and the collection, *"The eSmith Short tales: Fables & Stories from Fairytale Land,"* are available in all major outlets and on Amazon. In another life, he has had stories and poems published by *The Monarch Review, Gambling the Aisle, Sanskrit, Foliate Oak Literary magazine,* and *The Helix Literary Magazine.* Additional information is at *randywhitenow.online*

www.ingramcontent.com/pod-product-compliance
Lightning Source LLC
Chambersburg PA
CBHW070316120726
47910CB00007B/2503